Zico

Gatekeeper to the Unknown

Zico

Gatekeeper to the Unknown

B.G. Worner

Published by Tablo

Special thanks to the children who read the book during the editing process. Angus, Claudia, Eve, Georgie, Jade, Olivia, Riley, Skye, Toby and Zali — your feedback was valuable and welcomed.

TABLE OF CONTENTS

CHAPTER 1

WELCOME TO ROLDÃO

The east coast city of Roldão, in tropical Brazil, is about to gain another resident. Zico prays it won't be him. His parents are threatening to leave him at his grandpa's place for an extended holiday. There, he will need to fend for himself to survive.

Zico's mood is foul. Trapped in the compact car, the nineteen-hour bumpy trip through mountain ranges is torture. Similar stunts have been staged by his mum and dad before. This time, their antics are so far-fetched they are absurd.

Zico slouches deeper into the backseat. He hopes his father will turn the car around, putting an end to this charade. His jealous eyes hover over his sister, Taís, strapped into the plush baby seat like a precious jewel.

The pressure in Zico's head is building. His usually nimble mind is stuck on one frustrating thought: *Why is she the centre of the family's universe?* Just on cue, his mother turns and smiles lovingly at Taís, then grimaces at him. His eyes widen, asking a silent *what?* before shifting his spiteful gaze to the blur of the road.

Zico now recognises that back on their farm in the Amazon, he pushed his parents' patience too far.

On the outskirts of town, right next to a vandalised 'Roldão' sign, the handover takes place. A firm shove from his father propels him toward the grim man.

'This is your Grandpa Fonso,' his father says.

The meeting is short, uncomfortable, and without emotion. Zico witnesses little love between the two men.

Always the strategist, Zico's mind whirs with ideas of playing the nice boy with Mum and Dad. This tactic might get him back in the vehicle. As much as he wants to say *you won, you got my attention!* pride makes him bite his tongue.

Too late! A hasty embrace and kiss on each cheek from his mother, two stern words from his father, 'Grow up!' Reality hits. Tires burning, the family car speeds off into the sunset.

Bitter tears sting Zico's eyes as he stares up at Fonso. Jaw clenched, he shrugs his shoulders, pretending to be cool. Then, he makes a show of strolling casually to the car. It is one of those fancy BMWs. He has never seen one in real life but refuses to share his delight.

Zico stands by the door, rooted to the spot. He clutches his suitcase like a shield against the unfamiliar surroundings. Head swivelling, he looks for his parents' car kicking up dust as they make their way back to him.

Fonso starts the engine and yells through the open car window, 'Are you coming or what?'

Zico kicks the gravel. Rock pellets spray the pavement, rat-ta-tat-tat. He mutters, 'Do I have an option?'

They accelerate from zero to one-hundred in moments, hurtling Zico into the unknown. The experience is overwhelming. Zico's head is spinning with way too many unanswered questions for a twelve-year-old know-it-all.

How long will I be here?
Is he really my grandpa?
Why didn't he say, 'Look at you, I'm so happy to see you'?

Why did we meet him out of town?

Is he an accomplice to my parents' trick?

With the sun rapidly going down, and the neighbourhoods getting poorer by the minute, it is scary. Zico doesn't let it show.

Fonso speeds through the cramped streets, steering erratically. They enter a dark laneway and skid to a standstill. He switches the engine off, grabs Zico's bag, and waves him to hurry up. Zico scampers to catch him. From the shadows, several teenagers approach the vehicle. They arrogantly take possession of it, sinking into the soft leather seats.

Zico stutters, 'You left the keys in the car.'

Fonso acknowledges with a nod. 'You're switched on. I like it.'

Zico protests, 'But they're stealing your car!'

Shaking his head, Fonso chuckles. 'That's not my car. It was already stolen.'

Stunned, Zico turns back. The gang reverses the BMW out of the laneway, almost crashing into traffic. He cranks his head skyward, staring at Fonso with the world's widest eyes.

Fonso levels his gaze at him. 'Let's just call it valet service.'

They reach the steep cable car operation, empty except for two cigarette-smoking, tattooed guards. They are respectful toward Fonso, greeting him as Patrão (Boss).

One of them turns to the boy. 'So, you must be Zico?'

Head bobbing, Zico is uncertain if he is in awe or dreads the familiarity shown by this hulk.

The ride takes them high up the rock wall. They pass shacks made from shipping containers. The buildings cling to the cliff edge in peril of collapse. He has never seen anything like this before. In one shed a dozen people sit on top of each other, eyes glued on a football match. Further up, an old man squatting on a toilet, waves at them. Zico's jaw almost bounces off his chest.

Unable to avert his eyes, the human zoo captures his full attention. A man and woman argue. A teenager throws a flimsy mattress against a wall. An old lady cooks with a waiting family hungrily eyeing the stove.

As the ground shrinks away, the tightly packed homes so close to his face, stun Zico. One shack sits atop another, few with glass in the windows. Loose aerial cables and washing lines spider-web the village. He imagines that living here is like getting stuck in one of those elevators seen in the movies. Claustrophobic, with way too many people squeezed in.

Fonso studies Zico's reaction to his community's way of life.

Zico asks, 'Do you live here as well?'

Fonso points to the top of scaffolded houses, one hundred metres above where they were standing a minute ago. 'Yes, but we've got the penthouse.'

Zico continues to survey the stack of tin boxes, stepping up the cliff. 'What's a penthouse?'

'Uninterrupted views with no one looking into your business,' Fonso explains with a chuckle in his voice.

The rattling cable car reaches its destination and locks into a deadbolt. Another tattooed guy opens the safety barrier. This one's face is even more unfriendly than those of the guys' below. Zico shudders at the sight of him. The muscle-bound man lunges forward, 'Boo!' Zico jumps back, rocking the cabin.

Fonso raises his hand, glaring at the prankster. 'What are you doing? He's a farm boy, from the Amazon. He's new to this neighbourhood. This is how you welcome him?'

A sheepish look followed by a quick, 'Sorry Patrão,' is offered.

A hand-chiselled walkway is interrupted by a massive metal grilled gate. The passage is sandwiched between the cliff and a few houses sitting behind the barricade. At the far end of the path, the steep rock face wraps around a red container, the pinnacle of the community.

Fonso punches several numbers into the digital lock at the gateway. Two fit-looking security guards, slouching on milk crates, acknowledge him.

Zico stands, gob-smacked, in the middle of an open-spaced, modified double shipping container. Fonso throws his bag on a cushioned door-less wardrobe. The strange alcove baffles Zico. It is stuffed with shirts that hang carelessly on coat hangers. A large drawer forms the base. Several ratty cushions are piled so high, they almost touch the clothes.

Zico's eyes wander over the tired-looking place. To the left is an open kitchen with filthy pots and plates, cluttering the sink. A small table in the centre of the room is occupied by three chairs and an old checkers set. The shower separates the bedroom and living room. It is surrounded by a transparent curtain, decorated with blue fish and bubbles, which offers no privacy.

The bed is vertically secured to a wall to save space. A massive flat-screen TV is bolted to the container. Cables disappear into a small hole in the corrugated metal.

Taking in his surroundings, Zico wonders where the restroom could be. He worries he may have to pee in a pot or out the window.

On cue, Fonso asks, 'Do you need the toilet?'

Zico shakes his head.

In one swoop, Fonso whisks all his shirts off the rod, throwing them on the table. He checks the bolt-slide is fastened on the inside of the wardrobe. Satisfied, he points invitingly to the bunk, 'Your quarters.'

Zico's head whips from the wardrobe to his grandpa and back.

'You heard me; you're sleeping in there. Let's chit chat in the morning to work out what's what. Enough for now. Sleep well.'

Numbly, Zico accepts his situation. Fonso turns and heaves one end of the bed. He lowers it to a horizontal position and crashes heavily on top of it. Before Zico settles on his bunk, the lights go out. It is pitch-black.

Fonso's voice rumbles the air. 'Welcome to Roldão, Zico.'

Zico finds it embracing and terrifying at the same time. A silent tear trickles down his cheek.

He whispers, 'Good night, Grandpa.'

The light flicks on. Fonso sits in the middle of his bed, ramrod straight. He is shocked to his core by the unexpected title.

'Listen, kid, don't make me older than I am. I go by Patrão. My full name is Afonso Aloisous Caiman-claw Ruas. To keep it simple, you can call me Fonso.'

The light is extinguished, as is the conversation.

★ ★ ★

The sun enters through the east-facing window, next to Zico's bunk-robe. The kettle whistles long after Fonso returns it to the stovetop. He faces his coffee mug full of steaming brew. Taking a sip, he burns his tongue and sets the cup down. With two long strides, he crosses the room and shakes Zico awake.

'Good morning, Zico.'

'Morning Grand... Fonso.'

Zico props himself against the wardrobe's upright. Fonso smiles slyly. He leans over Zico, unhinging the bolt that locks the bunk's back panels together.

'Hold on. You're in for a surprise!'

The doors swing-out with one sweeping push. Bright, blinding sun rays fill the frame. Zico and Fonso are dangerously close to the edge of the bunk. It lines up with the cliff wall, a hundred metres high. The pressure of Fonso's hand on Zico's shoulder calms his shaking body.

Fonso beams, 'Didn't I tell you; we've got the penthouse!'

Panic about the steep drop turns into hesitation. The beauty of the natural environment below captivates Zico. A forest is embedded in a crater, abutting the ocean.

'Wow, that is amazing.'

Fonso nods, 'And, it's all for free.'

'What do you mean?' Zico asks.

Fonso beckons Zico to follow him. They walk barefoot through the messy room to the front door. Looking around, Zico realises they are standing on top of the village. Fonso points to the line where the clifftop meets the sky. 'The people who live above us will pay their whole life for that view.'

They stroll to a gap between the house and the cliffside. Zico discovers a generous outdoor courtyard. Fonso cocks his head toward an adjacent room. A fire-engine-red garden hose wheel is secured to the wall.

'The bath, shower, and toilet are in there. This room stays tidy, no matter what!'

Zico is relieved by Fonso's seriousness. The rest of the place is a disaster zone when it comes to housekeeping.

'That room is the future, the house is the past,' Fonso states.

Bladder ready to burst, Zico sprints to the door, skidding to a stop as he enters the room. His mouth is wide open, just like his sparkling eyes.

Zico stares at a brand-new, modern bathroom. The oasis is naturally lit by skylights. The bathtub is so big it looks more like a pool. It rests next to the floor-to-ceiling window, with views of the ocean. A wall-spanning mirror reflects the view. The toilet hangs low on the wall like a sculpture. Zico is almost too scared to pee for fear of missing the bowl. After use, he polishes it with tissues.

Stepping outside, Zico turns back to mind map this magnificent experience. He wonders, *how can a bathroom be so palatial, while everything else here is such a dump?*

Zico and Fonso eat breakfast in the courtyard. It overlooks the scenic forest and ocean with its white-capped waves. To the right, if Zico stretches and peeps around the corner, he can catch a glimpse of the cliffside town.

'What did your parents tell you about me?' Fonso asks.

Zico recognises an accusing edge. He stops mid-chew with a mouthful of cereal, and blurts, 'Nothing.'

Fonso nods sternly. 'They ever mention me?'

A reluctant conspirator, Zico shares, 'Not even when I asked about you.'

Fonso locks eyes with Zico like they are in a staring contest. 'Ask me.'

Full of apprehension, Zico utters, 'Ask what?'

Fonso's voice is gravelly. 'What do you want to know about me? This is your one shot at it.'

Zico thinks for a moment, then pulls a notepad from his pocket. He flicks through the pages, which makes Fonso uneasy.

'What are you? A reporter? The police?'

Studying one particular reference, Zico hesitates. 'Why don't you and Dad get on, and how come this is the first time we've met?'

Fonso shoves his chair back, relaxing into the seat. He chuckles, 'You need notes for this?'

For the next hour, Zico bonds with his grandpa as he explains the past and present. It is complicated, just like any other family, Zico realises. The falling out was because his father disagrees with Fonso's life of uncertainty.

Fonso assures Zico the community he leads functions by rules and regulations. It may not run under the traditional rule of law, but this works to his advantage. Importantly, this house is a crime-free zone, and lies will not be tolerated.

There is a central question that Zico wants Fonso to explain. A slight tremble and cheeks flushed red broadcast his hesitation. Closing his eyes, he swallows. Then, he looks up at Fonso. 'Why did I end up here? You've had nothing to do with me before, so why are you my Patrão now?' All the while Zico holds Fonso's gaze, challenging his opponent to buckle.

'To teach you a lesson of what's real and what's not,' Fonso responds. 'This is your chance to connect with family. I think, I can share with you my experiences so you understand what's important, what's right, what's wrong. Hopefully, you'll be a better person for it. What do you think?'

Unfolding his arms, Zico offers his hand to seal the agreement. He appreciates the honesty in which the deal was struck. 'So, what's to know about this place?'

Fonso pushes all breakfast items aside. 'You need to learn fast how this neighbourhood works.' He dips his finger into Zico's leftover cereal. Using the mushy remnants, he draws four parallel lines on the table-top. From right to the left he names the spaces, 'Ocean, Deep Forest, Cliffside Village, Precious Above the Sea.' He squirts a dollop of honey in Cliffside Village. 'This is our place in society.'

Fonso cleans his sticky fingers on his shirt. Zico stares at him.

'What?' Fonso challenges.

Zico murmurs, 'You do a lot of things differently, not the way you're supposed to.'

'What do you want to do about it?'

Filled with shame, Zico lowers his eyes. Brown knuckles turn white from his grip on the table. Chin tucked in, he bites his lip before peeking at his grandpa.

'Exactly. Nothing. Now let's talk about matters that are really important.'

Fonso waves his hands theatrically as he explains his community's set up. 'Down there is the centre of our little universe, the Deep Forest. As you can see it is shaped like a salad bowl. Actually, it is the top of a once mighty fire-spitting volcano. The place is haunted and those who enter never return. We all accept this fact.'

Zico hangs on Fonso's every word.

'So many stories, rumours, and myths,' he continues. 'If someone enters the forest, the volcano will erupt, wiping out the district. At best, it will make the person disappear to appease the spirits.'

One eyebrow pulls upward in a question mark before Zico rolls his eyes.

'You may think it's superstitious, but we all believe it. It works and it keeps everyone safe. I know people — for real — who haven't come back.'

Fonso points around the house and below to the cramped sheds.

'This cliffside town is called Nothing Forever by others, but not by us,' he emphasises. 'I call it the Village of Hope because that is all we've got. We are not rich in money, but life. We exist outside the flag.'

Zico wants to say something, but before he can form a word, Fonso rattles on.

'We are the illegals. This entire town is built without approval. It used to be the dumping ground for shipping containers. After a while, they became shelters and evolved into organised chaos. The buildings, electricity, water, sewer system — everything you see — is not meant to be here. But it is.' Fonso straightens, jutting out his chin. 'And, so are we.'

Fonso's finger stabs the air several times in the direction of the clifftop. 'Up there, are the people in power. We can't see them, and they definitely don't want to see us, meet us, or talk to us.'

Zico is puzzled. 'Huh?'

'Their villas are set back so their world is undisturbed. They have magnificent views of the forest and ocean, but not the poor village. We are separated by walls, money, culture, police, ideas and knowledge.' Fonso pauses. 'There are three things that unite us. One: we support our national football team. Two: we never enter each other's world. Three: we never ever set foot in the Deep Forest. Now, is that clear?'

'Understood,' Zico confirms.

'The rest, you can work out for yourself. I'm not a social worker. So, listen. We have spirited neighbours, the best you can get. You will blend in and not upset anyone. My house is a safe haven. The entire village is aware you're here. That doesn't mean you are untouchable!'

Warning issued, Fonso gets up and disappears into the bathroom, leaving Zico to plot his adventures.

CHAPTER 2

ZICO'S WORLD

Later that morning, with Fonso off doing who knows what, Zico is alone in the house. His mood swings like a pendulum. One minute, he is happy-go-lucky with the freedom he has found. The next, he resents being off-loaded.

Zico wonders whether his parents miss him. He grunts harshly. 'Nah. If they don't miss me, I don't miss them. I'm my own boss now and I'll make the most of it.'

Independent at last, he breaks away from his mother's strict rules. The neatly packed suitcase stays on the floor, untouched.

His eyes wander the room, landing on the fridge. He saunters over to it and inspects what's on offer. Grabbing the milk, Zico karate kicks the door shut. A huge effort is required to find anything clean. He examines a mug and spoon in disgust.

Zico lights the gas, sparking a burst of flame. Then, he throws open the cupboard, searching for his beloved chocolate powder. When he finds the hiding place, he grimaces. *This low-grade excuse for chocolate is not up to my standards.*

Zico slumps back on the bunk. 'Huh, Village of Hope,' he sneers. 'Is Fonso for real? Nothing Forever is nothing like the resorts on TV. Nothing Forever is a waste of time. What a rip-off!'

Zico rolls over and gazes outside. The Deep Forest beckons. He murmurs, 'Maybe it's not a rip-off after all, but it is forbidden.'

His thoughts wander to what everyone is doing at his farm. Edging toward the window, Zico stretches his neck to check where the sun is. He figures it is around eleven in the morning.

Zico focuses his mind's eye. His home is at Tocantins in the Amazon Basin. A river system snakes around the property. His father's voice is in his head, *6 hectares are ample to earn a living.*

The little house floats off the ground, keeping reptiles and cane toads out. The gigantic satellite dish sits on the roof like a wide-brimmed hat. It is an uncommon luxury in these parts.

Three sheds stand a short distance from the house. A fork lifter, tractor, trailers, drums, and empty palettes are scattered around. The proud rooster struts while the chickens peck the dirt, looking for tasty treats. Curled up in the shade of the porch are the dog and cat.

A few hundred metres of a tight dirt track drifts downhill. This stretch slices the plantation into two sections. It connects the buildings to the public road.

By 11am at the farm, half the day is gone. He closes his eyes, winding the clock back for a wake-up call.

Dawn is announced by the rooster — 'cock-a-doodle-doo'. The crowing goes on and on, all year. *Wow!* Zico realises he slept in today. He cannot ever remember doing that before! He wonders if his lazy start was due to yesterday's boring trip. Or perhaps, because the rooster's maddening crow didn't reach his penthouse window.

Benício, their farmhand, lives in a nearby shed. He is responsible for the livestock. A scream from Zico's father to do the chores prompts him to feed the chicks. Once fed, the old rooster and his father shut up.

When they are not working, everyone fusses over Taís. She doesn't even do anything interesting.

Zico pulls out all stops to get his parents' attention. He tells jokes, turns magician, and cuts more cacao than ever, but he receives little pay-off.

What does a kid need to do to get noticed? Emotions out of control, mischief becomes his friend. Finally, Mum wants to talk, but only about his poor grades. She isn't interested in the cause.

One of Benício's chores is to collect fresh milk. The milkman leaves the bottles at the gate, two-hundred metres downhill from the house. Taís' wail is ear piercing. The wait for milk triggers chaos in the house.

Zico's father shaves, usually cutting himself, then showers. On a good day, he is singing, on a bad day, he is growling. While his mum makes breakfast, Zico sorts his schoolbag. She tells him off for not doing this chore the night before. With Taís around, things are awful. Dishes are often smashed in temper.

Zico multi-tasks, dressing in his school uniform while chomping on a banana. Black shoes, white socks, black shorts, and a yellow polo shirt. Hats are optional.

Felipe Santos, the local government representative, wields influence in the capital. He loves a crusade. The neighbouring town, Perda de

Fé, is chipping student uniforms. The device dobs on kids who skip class. Adults think it is clever, kids think it's crazy. Santos is rallying to introduce the scheme at Zico's school.

Walking through the plantation to the road is the best part of Zico's day. Things grow right before his eyes in the Amazon. There is always something new to discover. When it rains, Benício gives him a lift on the tractor. Zico takes control of the steering wheel while the one-armed farmhand shifts the gears for the trip. Branches scratch at them as they putter along the dirt track.

At the end of the driveway, a hut offers shelter. Zico's father built it over many days, after tending the farm. He even carved a bench from a Kapok tree.

The bus service is meant to pick him up at 8am weekdays. The operation is hit-and-miss. Time management in Brazil's remote regions is not the highest priority. The driver is a farmer in need of extra money. With chores to be done every morning, he often runs late. This is accepted by students who smile politely at him while making fierce complaints behind his back.

Zico is the first to be picked up and last to be dropped off. This is the only means for rural kids to get to town. Forty pupils presided over by one teacher receive a basic education. Now the government-funded bus ride is indefinitely suspended. A recent fire rumoured to be the work of an arsonist destroyed the school. With no teacher available, classroom learning is denied.

Zico tenses as he recalls the moment everything changed.

Parents petitioned the government to introduce online schooling. They celebrated their victory, but that solution created its own problems. Only half the farms have reliable Wi-Fi. Most children have to wander their estates, hoping to find a signal.

Thinking back to his school friends' plight, Zico laughs. Paulo climbed a wobbly stack of crates in an attempt to connect to data. Ravi had to lean from the second storey window with his laptop strapped to a wooden plank. While Luiz did his schoolwork high up on a silo.

Ingenuity kicked in. Zico gathered farming equipment and fence posts from the field. He built a treehouse several metres above the ground, near the sheds. Then hung a cardboard sign on the door: *Do not disturb — I'm studying.*

His learning hub became a lesson in non-compliance. Pretending to do schoolwork taught him his parents had no clue. Zico spent hours gaming instead of working on the subjects set by the Academic Board.

One bright blue day, this venture came to an end. His father bulldozed the treehouse. Even stoic Benício felt sorry for Zico who was forced to witness the demolition.

Detained in the house, Zico tried to sneak out before the two-thirty clock-off time. For once, his mum's non-stop fussing over Taís worked to his advantage. His unwanted invisibility cloak enabled him to escape to the forest.

Zico imagines himself there, now. Tree climbing is his second favourite thing to do. In the treetops he swings through the branches, cutting cacao. Way below, Benício leans to the left to counter balance his missing limb. He teeters and struggles to catch the black gold in the over-flowing basket.

Black gold is chocolate that originates from cacao beans. Zico's parents grow the forastero variety. It makes the strongest flavour of all — a source of family pride.

His father always tells him how farming cacao to make chocolate helps the environment. The ecosystem is supported by planting sustainable agro-forests of native cacao trees. Rather than burning the rainforest, harvesting cacao keeps their habitat intact. It generates enough income to live well, compared to others.

By sunset, Zico is ready to collapse. Cable TV captures his imagination with glimpses of an otherwise unknown world. His friends hang on every word when he narrates his favourite shows. Zico drifts into a deep sleep until the rooster crows the next morning — 'cock-a-doodle-doo'. Another day in Zico's life on the farm begins.

He lives the same routine Monday to Saturday. To keep good things coming, every Sunday they visit the church. Zico reluctantly follows his parents' ritual to pray for forgiveness.

A strong, cold wind-gust sweeps up from the crater. It blasts into Zico's face, snapping him back to the present. He thinks, *maybe the family needed to be more genuine when praying for pardon, then they wouldn't be in this current predicament.* 'Seriously,' he mutters, 'how much more can someone pray?'

Without knocking, two overweight carpenters enter Fonso's house. They struggle to carry a solid double-thick glass panel.

The older man wheezes, sucking in a breath. 'Clear the bunk!'

Zico is startled by the intrusion. Seeing the man's legs buckle beneath his weight, prompts Zico to react. He flings the cushions across the room. They arc over the kitchen, catching the flickering flame on the stovetop. It doesn't take long for them to ignite and set the room ablaze.

The panicked carpenters drop the glass. Zico hastily screws the faucets in the shower. Built-up dirt and rust allow only a trickle of water to get through. Turning the taps full throttle, the pipes rattle and shudder. They release an unbearable squeal. Pressure mounting, the showerhead explodes off its pipe, penetrating the fridge like a spear. Water gushes on the floor.

The workmen evacuate, dragging Zico with them. Outside, the men cough and splutter, shaking their heads in surrender. Zico grabs the garden hose and rushes to the house. He blasts torrents to tame the wild fire.

Just as the flames become manageable, Fonso and his guards arrive. Fonso drops his bag and races over to Zico. He bends and snaps the hose in his fist, choking the flow.

With a slight tremble, Zico faces him. He twists the water tap off unsure what to expect, but bracing himself for what's to come. The carpenters hover, greedily anticipating a reaction. The silence seems endless; it is excruciating. Zico wonders, *what's the consequence for burning down the Patrão's house?*

Zico is no stranger to the turmoil generated by stuff-ups. His default position is to cover up until it is no longer an issue. But not owning up makes uncertainty certain. Still, this is Zico's preferred tactic.

The problem is, someone always finds out. This triggers an emotional response in the name of teaching him a lesson and a protest by him when the punishment is handed out. Disappointment, screaming, shouting, tears, and slamming of doors complete the cycle. The drama is performed by either him or his parents.

Even if it's a bad rap, the rules are for a kid to comply. In the end, love wins over. Then, he settles in to wait for something else to go wrong.

Zico recognises this set of circumstances is different, especially with armed guards present. The needle on the trouble-meter hits catastrophic. No excuse can save him.

Fonso paces through the smouldering mess. He checks the glass panel before directing his gaze at the quivering carpenters. His deliberate silence and controlled movements are nerve-wracking and well-orchestrated. With a hint of a frown, Fonso turns back to the new window. Everyone holds their breath, waiting for his judgement.

The pacing stops when he reaches Zico, who still grips the dripping hose. At the touch of Fonso's hand on his shoulder, Zico jumps.

Drumming his fingers on Zico's shoulders, Fonso declares, 'Burn, baby burn.'

Nervous laughter erupts, defusing the tension. It dawns on Zico that Fonso never behaves the way you expect from an adult. He snorts a laugh that doesn't stop.

Fonso senses his awkwardness. 'The only thing that matters is that you're okay. And you are, right?'

The tension in Zico's body melts away. He briefly bows his head.

'The window is in one piece and the bunk is as solid as ever. The rest was up for renovation anyway.' Fonso directs his mob into action.

Like a python, Zico wraps his arms around Fonso, squeezing gratitude into him.

CHAPTER 3

THE YELLOW BALL

The sun is setting behind the Precious Above the Sea clifftop community. Distorted shadows of high-rise buildings stretch over Nothing Forever. Fonso's crew assemble a medium-sized, grey tent next to the courtyard table. Zico scrambles to help.

A working bee extends from inside the house to the gate. They strip the charred building bare, stacking the wooden floorboards outside. Surrounded by a makeshift protective barrier, the glass panel leans against the bathroom wall.

Fonso paces the compound, focus split between the nonstop ringing of his mobile phone and worksite progress. The renovation creates excitement and demonstrates how the village pulls together in tough times. It does help that Fonso is

Nothing Forever's Patrão. On top of that, the warm summer weather raises everyone's spirit.

With shadows morphing into darkness, the exhausted tradies retire for the day. Fonso and Zico enjoy the serenity of their newfound outdoor life. The star-studded night sky puts on a glittering show. They gather around the fire pit which is fuelled by old floorboards. A dozen sticks speared with beef flank grill over the flames. The aroma is tantalising. Zico dips the barbecued skewers into the tangy Cilantro Chimichurri sauce. A flavour worth savouring.

'So, how was your day?' Zico asks.

'I've learned over time you have to tear down to create. The problem is, waiting makes me restless,' Fonso confides.

Eyes cast down, Zico gives an apologetic smile.

Fonso hones in. 'Look, I know the fire was an accident. Don't worry. I started the renovation a while ago, with the bathroom. The rest was going to happen at some point. Now, the job will be finished in the next two days. We'll be back in the house before the rain comes. In the meantime, we sleep alfresco. Have you ever slept in a tent?'

'No, never. This will be fun,' Zico chirps. 'But how comfortable is sleeping on the ground for someone your age?' He quickly corrects himself, 'And, position.'

Fonso snorts a laugh. 'We could stay anywhere. Right next door, they would've moved out for us. In fact, they offered exactly that. Or we could go to a posh hotel.' Fonso shakes his head. 'No. I belong here.' He casts his eyes over the campsite. 'What beats this? I haven't slept outdoors in years. Can't even remember the last time.'

Zico is comfortable with the silence that settles over them while Fonso experiences the rarity of questioning his own decisions.

'Why? Do you want to sleep somewhere else?'

Lightning-fast Zico cuts in, 'No, no way. This is so cool here.'

Smiling broadly, Fonso nods his agreement.

They sink deep into their chairs. Zico drags a blanket across his knees. The flicker and crackle of the flames is hypnotic, and mind and body re-charging.

Coming out of his trance, Zico's confidence is restored. He asks, 'What really happened between you and Dad?'

'We live different lives,' Fonso responds.

'That's all?'

'Yes, but that difference is a lot,' Fonso says.

'What are the differences?'

'Well, the easy ones are about the city versus the Amazon. In the jungle people are in sync with the environment whereas here, we exist off the land. There, people work hard to make a living from cacao, here we get by, doing all kinds of things.'

Zico teases, 'Like stealing BMWs?'

Fonso squirms, uneasy with Zico's probing. He is not used to answering to anyone. The last time he got into it, he lost his son. Now, his grandson's curiosity is pushing boundaries.

'I heard Dad talking to you on the phone one day. He mentioned other crimes.'

Fonso breathes in deeply, blowing out hard. 'I guess that's where the Q and A ends.'

Zico shrinks at the barb. Put in his place, he is confused by Fonso's dismissal. One-minute Fonso treats him like an adult – well, not exactly equal, but respected. Then, when an awkward topic is raised, he is fobbed off like a silly school kid.

Fonso senses Zico's disappointment. He changes tack. 'Your Dad and I are united by two things. One: you Zico. Two: an oversized satellite dish.'

Zico cranks his head, eyeing the roof. Getting up for a better view, the size of the monster makes him whoop with joy. 'Wow, just like ours,' Zico exclaims.

Amused, Fonso lets out a hearty chuckle.

Zico flops back down next to the fire, tension drifting away. He thinks, *maybe, just maybe, someone gets me.*

'Why don't you stroll around the village tomorrow,' Fonso suggests. 'Whatever you do, don't leave the hillside. At the bottom to the right, just below the gates, another neighbourhood starts. They have their own rules. You're an outsider — a target. On the other side of the cliff is the federal prison. I'm telling you, you never want to enter that place,' he chuckles.

Zico cracks up.

'This cliffside community is an amazing labyrinth. Plenty of stairs, open doors, people, and lots of problems. It's raw, Zico. I'm not going to sugar-coat the facts. The code for the security gate is four, seven, eight, one, then press OK. Repeat it!'

Zico recites, 'Four, seven, eight, one.'

Fonso studies Zico. 'Good. Now, are you up for it?'

'Yeah. Sure am. I did plan to walk around today before...' Zico chokes on the thought of the fire.

Fonso scruffs Zico's hair. 'I talked to your dad earlier.'

'You did?' Zico is eager for information.

'They miss you, they really do! I guess you all need to start appreciating each other more. I've learned you only know the value of things once they're lost. Sad, isn't it?' Fonso's eyes water as his mind wanders.

Zico cautiously interrupts his thoughts. 'What else did he say?'

'Ahh, he didn't say much. Then I mentioned the fire and he freaked out. I told him you're safe here. Safer than in the Amazon, that's for sure. Then he asked me a bunch of strange questions.'

Zico holds his breath, hanging on to every word.

'How the blaze started? Who was there? What part did you play? Your father went on and on. I guess he was worried.' Fonso offers a tight smile. 'The conversation was too much like an inquisition for my liking.'

Zico nods warily.

'Accidents happen and good things have already eventuated from it.'

Zico glances at Fonso. 'Maybe,' he mumbles.

Fonso's craggy face softens as he offers a small smile. 'I know today was difficult. We will get through it.' He pauses. 'Don't waste your time on worry and grudges. The past is gone. You can't do anything to change that. Focus on the present. I want you to discover the colosseum.'

'There's a colosseum? Here?' Zico scoffs.

'Not one like you imagine. Like the one in Rome where gladiators fought.' Fonso reconsiders, 'Well, actually, it is a lot like that, except animals don't get hurt. It's a basketball court with football goals, surrounded by houses and some fencing. You know what a tinder box is, Zico?'

Wide-eyed, Zico shakes his head. 'Nope.'

'A tinder box is something easily ignited. The colosseum is a hotbox of emotions.'

As Fonso describes the sporting arena Zico visualises it. Caged by broken mesh, the playing field is carved out by the walls of the surrounding houses. Sheds, windows, balconies, and lookouts are packed with people of all ages. The setting is loud and intense.

A referee monitors the action from a nearby balcony. He is armed with a whistle and a flag, one side red, the other yellow. A kid operates the improvised scoreboard with sand-filled beer bottles broadcasting the result.

Fonso explains, 'Everyone hangs out at this crazy

social hub. If you're lucky, they might let you join a match.'

'Who plays?' Zico wonders out loud.

'Anyone who wants to be someone,' Fonso booms. He pushes himself up from the chair and half-jogs to the tent. Fonso calls out, 'We stage a summer football comp. They battle, five a side, no subs. Teams play ten minutes each half.'

The tent is littered with loose items scattered about. Fonso rummages to find the bag he carried home earlier. Reclaiming his seat by the fire, Fonso presents the gift to Zico. He peers inside, a grin spreading across his face.

A custom-made, yellow, size four football, blows Zico away. He has never seen such a shiny ball, so new and made of real leather. He inhales its rich, almost sweet scent.

'This will help you to break the ice in the colosseum. Don't lose it. That's your first challenge,' Fonso warns. 'I've been to hell and back to get this for you. The company that supplies the Brazilian football team made it. It's a one-off and yours now.'

Zico jumps up and hugs Fonso.

A short while later, Zico settles into sleep with the yellow ball tucked in tight next to him. Fonso switches the torch off.

★ ★ ★

The next morning, tired and annoyed by unwanted noise, Zico slides up the zip to the outside world. The sky is blue and the wind is fierce. Peering through the flap, he spies on the army of carpenters, plumbers, and electricians. The workers fight over the little space in the house. Fonso is nowhere to be seen.

An envelope addressed to Zico is taped to the impressive ball resting beside him. Breaking the seal, he discovers 500 Reais (around $100 dollars). Zico reads the note.

Take what you think you'll need, then hide the rest.
Your bag is in the tent — brush your teeth.
Make sure you talk to the plumber before turning the water on.
No electricity today.
Don't do anything I wouldn't do — like start a fire.
The gate is open and guarded — if not, you know the code.

Zico removes a crisply folded piece of paper, revealing a hand-drawn map of the hillside village. It features a mess of little gateways, steps, and houses stretching out like tentacles. In the middle of Fonso's plan, the colosseum is marked by a rectangle. From the security gate, a dotted line zigzags to the social hub.

Changed and refreshed, Zico makes his way past the armed guards standing at the entrance. They greet him, but their eyes are glued on the yellow ball. One guard lets out a whistle. Zico holds his head high, triumphant. *Today is going to be a good day.* Everyone is finally paying attention to him.

Passing the guards, he enters the urban jungle and apprehension kicks in. The howling wind is tamed by the compressed buildings. Almost eerie. It is exactly how Fonso described the experience around the fireplace last night. The shack-like homes are of a much lower construction standard compared to what is behind the gate.

The houses are packed and stacked tin cans. He remembers Fonso telling him they are fitted-out with salvaged or stolen materials. Over the years, people added extensions to accommodate their growing families. The collective outcome is a quirky charm.

Zico marvels at the buildings. Painted in a rainbow of colours, they sparkle like a kaleidoscope in the summer sun. The structures are random, without any planning. Only the cogwheel cable car marks a straight line from the bottom to the top. To the left, the volcano's crater, home to the Deep Forest, cuts into the cliff. Glimpses of the stunning high-rise villas at the clifftop show the scope of disparity between rich and poor.

The narrow laneways are an obstacle course, teaming with people. Nobody seems to care he is being ricocheted around. Without warning, a group of teenagers fly past him on mountain bikes. They are hell-bent on being the first down the winding stairway. Stumbling through the maze, he is fascinated by the lack of proper roads. There is no sense of order.

He recalls Fonso reminiscing about how he gained and retained power. Electricity, running water, and a sewer system was an unexpected luxury for the shanty town. His army of skilful fixers can do anything, free of charge, for the people. As long as they keep building extensions and mending things, Fonso will be the Patrão. What Zico cannot work out is where the money comes from to pay the workers.

Zico gawks into every open door. Statues and artefacts of the Candomblé faith stare back at him. The wooden carvings worshipped resemble African bodies clothed in Middle Eastern patterns. Thanks to Sunday morning church sessions back home, he is familiar with the traditions and beliefs. The faith's deep roots run back to when slaves were forced to settle in Brazil. The highlight of their ritual is an African-Brazilian dance.

He thinks about Candomblé's culture and how it honours the gods. Zico smiles, remembering the jubilation he felt during the dance around the fire last night. He has never seen so many tributes. This community's heart and soul is bound by religious and social organisations and their celebrations.

Zico rotates the map to get his bearings. Navigating the arched passages, winding through houses, he reaches his destination. Kids queue to clamber to the prime spectators' spot at the top of the colosseum's fence.

As Fonso predicted, it is a hothouse. A game is underway. Judging by the roar of the spectators, the match is fiercely competitive. Intent on getting closer to the action, Zico squirms his way between bodies, stepping on toes. It's no use. Crammed like piglets in a playpen, the incredible din of chatter, insults, and laughter, is exhilarating. In the crush of the crowd, Zico finds strength in his anonymity.

The sheen of the yellow ball attracts an eagle-eyed opportunist, perched above on a ledge. The boy swoops in, beckoning Zico to follow to a better vantage point. They disappear into a house, climb steep, rickety stairs, and emerge on the balcony.

Zico's eyes pop and his heart races. The view of the pitch and fans below is unobstructed. He imagines he is in a corporate box, watching the Brasileirão, the Brazilian professional football league. *What a spectacle!*

As the whistle blows for half time, Zico shouts encouragement. His lingering cheers alert others to the presence of an outsider. A buzz of anxious anticipation rumbles, followed by a thunderous silence. Almost everyone is staring and pointing at him. He stumbles back to escape their gaze.

A collective gasp rustles. A teenage boy scurries up the drainpipe and snatches the ball from Zico's trembling hands. He hurdles balconies before hauling himself to higher ground. Skin rippling, Zico screams, 'Nooo!'

A minute later the thief is on an adjacent roof. Hoisting the ball above his head like a trophy, he howls a victory cry. 'We've got a new ball!' With an almighty kick, he launches it into the sky.

The players jostle for position in the colosseum, ready to receive the pass. Kudos will be given to the player who gains possession of the yellow ball. A wind squall blows the ball way off its trajectory. Zico, the spectators, and the teams crane their necks, trying to follow its path. It is out of sight.

From the rooftop, the thief frowns his disappointment, his moment of glory short-lived. The ball drops over the crater into the Deep Forest.

The crowd murmurs, 'Where is it? Did you see where it landed?'

A whistle blasts. The referee yells, 'You can't miss what you've never had. Game on.'

Zico slinks away, shoulders slumped, head down, tears splashing his face. He glides his hand along the wall to steady himself. Turning into a dark alley, he squats down in grief. Zico's head is exploding, his whole body tense. Concentrating on his breathing, Zico is determined to control himself. He needs a plan.

Dragging his feet up the stairway to the gated compound, Zico is distraught. His stomach churns at the thought of telling Fonso he lost his precious gift. Three-quarters of the way up, he accepts time is up. There is no choice but to tell the truth.

He kicks a vase decorating the steps of a shed. It skitters across the path like a ball. Zico mutters, 'It's about the right size and shape.' Glancing around, he hesitates before stuffing it in his backpack.

Continuing up the walkway and past the security guards at the gate, he reassures himself all the way. *Not telling is not lying.*

As he arrives at the compound, Zico notices Fonso talking with the builders. Taking a deep breath, he forces a smile and waves as he strides toward the tent.

CHAPTER 4

THE MISSION

Handymen work frantically on the house. Benches are set up around the perimeter; each dedicated to a trade — electrical, plumbing and carpentry. They are like a colony of ants, united to convert scraps into a home.

With the inside gutted, a concrete floor is being laid. Interior fittings are stacked outside. The outdoor table is the workers' meeting and resting place.

Zico is preoccupied. He slouches against the rail in the one free corner of the courtyard. Eyes trained on the Deep Forest; he seeks inspiration. The gravity of his lost ball worries him. *If I stare long and hard enough, I'll find the answer.* Zico's concentration breaks with Fonso's approach.

'So, how did it go?'

His mind is blank for a split second. Zico blurts, 'Great.'

'Did you make any friends?' Fonso asks.

'No, not today.'

Eyebrows raise all the way to Fonso's hairline. 'And...'

Brain power restored. Zico adds, 'The hillside is a maze, just like you told me. The map helped a lot. I would've never found the colosseum or my way back. Naming the walkways would help.'

'What would we name them? In this neighbourhood, things change fast. What's a walkway today might be someone's bedroom next week.'

Zico's voice intensifies. 'Everyone is into Candomblé here. Much more than we are, back home. I thought we were religious!'

'Yeah,' laughs Fonso. 'Believing in Candomblé is extremely intense. The faith here is almost superstitious. Especially with the Deep Forest channelling the unknown factor of fate, fear, and magic.'

Zico now understands. Setting foot in the forest is sacrilegious. That's why no one goes there.

'Now tell me, was the ball a winner?' Fonso asks.

Zico reminds himself not to lie. Masterfully, he avoids the whole truth. 'It really made an impact.'

'Did you play?'

'Nah. I wanted to see the colosseum, which was amazing. To be honest, I'm better at watching than playing.'

Sensing Zico's insecurity, Fonso offers some guidance. 'Good comes from having a go. Some are better than others, but football here is about engagement. Nothing should stop you from chasing your own kind of greatness. The important thing is being comfortable with yourself!' He scruffs Zico's hair.

Hands shoved in his pockets, Zico offers a tight-lipped smile before looking away.

'Once the renovations are over, we'll kick that ball of yours,' Fonso enthuses.

Zico gives a one-shouldered shrug, licking his lips in dismay. He is grateful Fonso is called away to inspect the house and doesn't notice his discomfort.

Zico needs to find and recover the ball, pronto. *What's the chance? If another kid finds it, they'll keep it; the ball would be a badge of honour. But then again, it is so unique; who else but Fonso's grandson is the rightful owner. Surely that is an incentive to return it.*

Always the strategist, Zico thinks this puts the odds of getting the ball back in his favour. *How can I get the message out, without Fonso ever knowing?* Zico's brain is in overdrive. His thoughts are interrupted by the flash of yellow in the Deep Forest.

Tuning out everything around him, Zico concentrates on detecting movement. With eyes crinkled to slits, he zeroes in on the location where he spotted the glimmer. *Could that have been my ball?*

Looking around on the sly, he checks no one is watching him. Just in case, he repositions himself further along the courtyard. Zico continues his stakeout. He is about to write it off as wishful thinking when he spots a yellow pulse. *There's the ball!* Zico jumps back, pumping his fist in the air.

Triumph turns to defeat with the realisation that retrieval is impossible. He peeks through open fingers, eyes bulging at the streak of yellow.

Zico recognises the turbulent wind from this morning has dropped. 'Something or someone is playing with my ball,' he mutters.

Like a detective, he forces himself to take another investigative look. Zico racks his brain. 'What will Fonso do when he learns I lost the ball to the forest?'

Erratic pacing mirrors his state of mind until he spies binoculars on a cupboard. Within a blink of an eye, he grabs them. He has never used binoculars but is aware they make distant objects bigger. His father's voice is in his head: *never point the lenses towards the sun.* Positioned on the edge of the courtyard, Zico surveys the unknown territory.

The ocean is magnified so much he reaches out to touch the waves. He laughs at himself. Zico scopes the house and then the hillside village. He follows the containers, intruding on a woman shaving her legs. Lowering the glasses, Zico shakes his head.

He focuses on the prison tower to his left. This is the only structure within the complex that can be seen. No windows face the cliff but smoke wafts from the prison tower.

Honing in on what could only be the yellow ball, his vision is obscured. *What is that?* Zico zooms in on a brown paw protectively clamped on the ball. His mouth drops like a trap door suddenly released and snaps shut again.

A rough slap to the side of the head startles Zico. Dropping the binoculars, the leather strap bites into his neck. Ear ringing, he barely hears the workman yell at him. 'What are you looking at?'

Zico turns, heart jack hammering in his chest. He stammers, 'Nothing, just a, a, a bird.'

The man narrows his eyes, sizing up Zico. 'Just a pretty bird, eh?'

Tensing his muscles to stop the jitters, Zico's eyes flash in defiance. With a smug smile and shake of the head, the worker walks away. Zico is off the hook.

Attention back on the Deep Forest, he adjusts the dials. No matter how hard he tries, he finds no sign of movement. No yellow ball. No brown paw.

Mouth twisted and nose crinkled, Zico questions himself. *Was it an illusion?* He suspects in his desperation he invented the yellow ball whizzing through the trees. He kicks the railing, letting off steam.

Zico reasons he can either enter the forbidden place to retrieve the ball with no one ever knowing, or, it is in the community and will be returned to its rightful owner. Both scenarios rely on Fonso not finding out the ball was stolen. Zico understands this would not be pleasant for the thief and his family and being caught in a half-truth won't do Zico any favours either.

Without fail, the ball must be back, at the latest, by the day after tomorrow. This is when the renovations will be completed and when Fonso will play with him at the colosseum. The frantic pace of construction reminds him of a reality TV show. Only, this is really happening, right before his eyes.

Logical thinking tells Zico the yellow flash is his ball. *What harm can come from recovering it?* To settle his conscience, Zico justifies why he should go.

1. I am not superstitious so no spell will be cast on me.
2. I am innocently getting my ball back so even the saints, if they are present or real, will accept this as the right thing.

He argues with his superego. *The spirits will celebrate me for preserving the forest from the foreign object. Win, win, win. No consequences.*

Now he has to plan for a rescue mission that must remain undetected. He needs to be cunning like a coyote; smart and sneaky to make the raid and take him off the endangered list.

Zico sits at the outdoor table, surrounded by lunch- and tool-boxes, chewing his pen. He drafts his plan in scribbled handwriting in his notebook:

Create diversion — can't be missing
Wear green — can't be seen
Take backpack and water
Find tools — ladder or rope, string a few hundred meters

long, handsaw and hook, gloves
Descend quietly — must not be heard by a prison guard
Climb back
Never tell anybody

Zico strolls around the worksite, faking interest in what's going on. Eyes shifting, he scans the place for the items on his list, each one a necessity for mission success.

After the workmen leave, Zico uses the remaining floorboards to start a fire. He rubs his hands together, willing himself to sit still. With a quick lick of the lips, his grin is replaced with a mask of innocence.

Waiting for Fonso to arrive, Zico's eyes dart back and forth. He spots some rope exposed at his hiding place. He sprints across and covers it with a small rock. Zico detours, reassessing the distance to reach the top of the crater. It is really steep.

Checking for possible points of detection, he scopes the village and the far side of the cliff. *Couldn't find a more perfect spot!* Fonso's house sits on a different angle with the courtyard curving away from the village. He reckons the rope should be camouflaged.

Satisfied, he returns to the fire. Flicking through his notebook, Zico quietly reviews the catalogued items:

Mission — daytime three hours, easy.
No rain — perfect.
Excuse to disappear — going to wander around.
Don't mention football.
Green shirt, black shorts, backpack — tick, tick, and tick.
Rope — long and strong enough.
Handsaw and hook — done.
Gloves — way too big, but will do.
String — will go a long way.

Hearing the crunch of Fonso's footsteps, Zico stuffs his notes into his pocket in the nick of time.

Fonso dumps the groceries on the table. He circles the burning fireplace, eyes twinkling. 'What a nice surprise, Zico. Hope you're hungry. We're having grilled fish and potatoes.'

An hour later, under the Milky Way, Fonso and Zico are fed. A stray cat scavenges from the generous leftovers.

Fonso begins their evening conversation with his customary question. 'How was your day, Zico?'

'Interesting. Tomorrow, I'll spend a few hours on the hill. I don't like being around the builders. They think I'm a pest. Anyway, I've got the taste for discovery.'

Fonso nods his approval. 'I get that. One thing is for sure, we're back in the house in two days. Then, we kick your ball around at the colosseum. Where is the ball?'

Zico's heart skips a beat. 'Where nobody will find it! It's top secret.'

Fonso chuckles, 'Smart boy. In the end, you can only trust yourself, right?'

'Right!' Zico quickly changes topics. 'Wow, this renovation is speeding along.'

'Sure is. I've got no patience. I want everything now, and it better be good. See, I go by a very simple principle: whatever you say, you do. That way you end up ahead, eventually.'

'Why?' Zico pauses, 'I mean, why does it work that way?'

'Because reliability creates trust, which is hard to come by these days.'

Zico appreciates Fonso's wisdom. Gazing into the flames, he shares, 'This is a place of trust. The firepit. Shame, with the renovation speeding along, the firepit's days are numbered.'

Fonso recognises how their time around the fire brought them together. 'Won't happen. We'll get a proper fireplace installed,' Fonso declares.

'Really?'

'Consider it done!'

Shortly after sunrise, Zico is dressed in his camouflage clothes. He sits at the outdoor table, helping himself to a second serve of cereal and two bananas. His increased eating habits don't go unnoticed.

'There is a tomorrow, Zico,' Fonso assures him.

Almost choking on the banana, Zico splutters, 'I need energy today, lots of walking in the hills.'

'I find the steps take the oomph away,' Fonso says. 'By the way, where do you want the new fireplace?'

'Where it is! Don't you think so?' Zico asks.

Fonso agrees. As he walks off, he calls out, 'I'll be in and out all day. Don't do anything I wouldn't do.'

Zico makes certain the security gate closed after Fonso left. He rushes to the hiding place, moving rocks to uncover the equipment. Checking the sun's position, he starts organising his tools.

'Thirty minutes to set things up before the builders arrive,' he mutters.

Tying a knot at the end of the rope, Zico drags it around the edge of the cliff. He navigates the ledge, just wide enough for him to pass, making his way to the shallow cave. Zico threads the rope around a massive boulder. Tugging with all his strength to secure it, he almost loses his balance.

He steadies himself, fastens the rope, and tests it will carry his weight. Zico throws it over the cliff and watches it uncoil. To his dismay, the line dangles metres short of the crater.

Hugging the rockface, Zico takes tentative steps back to the courtyard. He confirms the string and the water bottle are in the backpack. Then, he peers down at the spot where he believes the ball is. *Well, the rope's an issue, but it's not too bad.* Zico almost talks himself into confidence.

Compared to Zico's other recent setbacks for carefully orchestrated plans, this is nothing. Sometimes things don't work the way they are intended. Like being king of his universe when he was the only child, before princess Taís came along. The treehouse was his substitute for school. Courtesy of his father, it didn't last long. A promise of misadventure on the farm landed him on his own in Nothing Forever.

These plans were torn up by others or by circumstance. Zico learned from his father, it's not what it is that matters, it's what you make of it that defines you. *Sound advice* , he thinks.

Zico pulls on the gloves, takes hold of the line, and swings his body over the edge. He wraps his legs around the rope, attempting a controlled descent. Quiet as a whisper, he lowers himself past the prison guard tower.

CHAPTER 5

THE DEEP FOREST

Zico's feet dangle a metre and a bit above the crater top. He is a drop away from his quest to rescue his ball. Letting go of the rope, he sinks knee-deep in pulverised sand.

His eyes are focused on the frayed rope-end, hanging well out of his reach. Grabbing it later to climb up the wall will be a massive challenge. Just like the unexpected test he now faces. The powder is sucking him under. He needs to act fast to avoid being buried in the shifting sand.

Zico pumps his legs as he pushes the sand away from his upper body. Something brittle is clawing at his waist. He furiously yanks the object and is repulsed by the touch. Even before he sees it, he understands it is a game-changer. A chill runs up his spine as he finds himself holding hands with a skeleton. Zico's cyes bulge like balloons ready to pop. He clamps his mouth shut to swallow the scream.

Five minutes of frantic wriggling releases Zico from the sinkhole. Flinging his backpack from his shoulders, Zico collapses on it. He bodysurfs, out-of-control, down the sandy crater. The fifty-metre slide is fast and furious. The impact is vicious with Zico and his improvised vehicle smashing into bushes.

Shaking in equal measure from terror and exhilaration, Zico whoops. Lightheaded and sweating buckets, he pats himself down from head to toe. A splattering of blood is on his shirt and his hands. The sharp, stinging pain on his face makes his eyes water. He touches his cheek tentatively, flinching when his fingers cross the raw, sticky edge of the wound.

Undeterred, he unhooks the handsaw from the backpack. Zico pulls the ball of string from the bag. He ties the end around a tree, before returning it to his kit.

Swinging the bag up, he catches it on his shoulder. Zico gauges the time from the sun. He does a three-sixty spin, scanning up and down for anything suspicious. Nothing. He reassures himself. *No rumblings, no upset spirits. What a lot of hoodoo voodoo.*

Zico cuts a path into the thick forest. He sweats profusely in the sauna-like environment. The wound has stopped bleeding; the bright red splotches on his t-shirt have darkened, taking on a brownish hue.

The crack of a branch snapping nearby stops him dead in his tracks. He strains his ears. The only noise he detects is his heartbeat. The eerie silence affects him. For the first time, he considers if this mission is foolish. Scared spitless, Zico fights the urge to run. He is determined to see this through.

Zico removes his backpack and takes a gulp from his water bottle. He scrutinises the landscape, then checks the string continues to map his path. His eyes follow the line disappearing into dense vegetation as he re-harnesses the bag.

One hour into his mission the sun has risen considerably; he assesses the sun like clockwork. Occasionally, he examines the network of algae, lichen, and moss, clinging to tree trunks.

Roldão is in the southern hemisphere. Flowerless green plants grow on the south side of the trees; whilst spiders prefer the opposite side. Naturally, this will be the other way around in the northern hemisphere. Zico learned this growing up in the Amazon. Direction can be established in many ways.

So deep in the forest, he relies on these life skills to locate his ball's estimated resting place.

Casing the undergrowth, he wonders how the tiny seedlings ever reach the monumental heights of the canopy. Zico stops at a statuesque, ancient looking tree and examines its twisting root system. It starts five metres above the ground to support the towering tree's weight. He traces his fingers over its rough surface, inspecting it for moss.

Zico slides off his backpack and climbs confidently to the top. He declares, 'I Zico, observer of nature, shall name you the Tree of Knowledge.'

He pushes some branches aside to establish his whereabouts. High up the cliff face, he recognises Fonso's house. To the left is the hillside township. To the right is the roof of the prison guardhouse.

I'm close. The ball must be somewhere here. Zico smiles, pleased with his progress. Optimism turns to fear. Right beneath him, tree branches rustle in the otherwise calm forest. Something big is moving around down there. Zico cannot work out where the sound is coming from. It is unsettling.

He descends, head swivelling, eyes darting. A nearby movement causes Zico to lose his grip. Literally! Legs and arms wheel. His downward slide becomes a backward roll, abruptly halted by a heavy crash. It almost knocks him out.

He stumbles to his feet. Shaking his head, he rids the stars dancing before his eyes. At blistering speed, he stuffs the scattered equipment in his bag. Zico staggers into the dense bush, fleeing the movement and noise.

Mad panic courses through him. Zico hurtles through the foliage, constantly watching his back. Something is out there. He trips, rolls, and falls, landing face down. Looking around, expecting the worst, he locates the yellow ball just out of reach. Digging his hands into the dirt, almost clenching it, water trickles from his eyes. *What a lucky achievement!* Exhausted, he crawls to his prized gift.

Halfway to standing, a thump in the chest sprawls Zico on his backside. He desperately clings to the ball. The hot funky breath of a furry beast blasts his nostrils. Zico falls back, his scared-stiff body digging into the ground. The jaguar's paw stamps down on the ball. It is a mismatched standoff. His attacker's throbbing neck veins, bared teeth, and angry squint render Zico frozen.

The wild cat is a beautiful specimen, twice Zico's size. Only he wishes he met him at a zoo from behind a safe zone. The animal stays put, glaring at him. Zico lets the ball roll away. The jaguar's eyes track its movement but his head remains still, ready to pounce. A glob of drool slinks from its jaw toward his face. Zico knows this is his end. He is about to be mauled.

Zico is upset with himself for letting his family down. The big cat is centimetres in front of his face. Reflected in its eyes is a flash of Zico's short life, full of mischief and resentment.

Squeezing his eyes shut, Zico waits for the king of the jungle to snuff him out. Nothing happens. He forces his eyes open. The jaguar blinks, imitating him.

Zico gasps. He must be hallucinating. Unable to stop himself, he raises his hand to touch the dark rosettes on its brownish-yellow fur. The jaguar nudges him, pushing his head into Zico's palm. Zico continues to stroke him just like he does with his pets back at the farm. He then pushes the ball to Zico.

Releasing his breath, Zico maintains his guard. He acknowledges this is a wild animal and jaguars like meat. Although he is on the skinny side, he is still a potential food source.

Zico reaches out with his left hand, feeling for the ball. He carefully pushes it away. The playful cat springs after it, nudging it back. As they roll the ball back and forth Zico plans how to get out of this dilemma.

He throws the ball as far as he can to test if there is time to flee. Within moments, the jaguar kicks it joyfully back, waiting for more. Just like an obedient dog.

Zico thinks, *running away may be an option, but where could I escape to?* He is on his own on the wild cat's turf. *Why should I run away? This creature is craving attention — something I can easily relate to.*

They play for half an hour before Zico registers the need to rush home. He grabs the ball, and crouches in front of the jaguar.

'Listen, I have to get back. I live up there.' Zico points to the sky and the outline of the clifftop. 'If I don't get home soon, I'm in trouble. I can come back another day.'

The jaguar's eyes blink. Understanding confirmed. Patting his new friend, Zico says, 'I can try to come back another day. You know what, I will come back to play with you.' He is rewarded with a purr for the first time.

Squatting down, Zico stuffs his belongings in his backpack. Quick as a flash, he does an about-face, pulling everything out again. He rummages through the contents in a desperate search for the ball of string. This is the insurance policy to find his way back.

The jaguar senses Zico's panic and snuggles into him.

Zico pats him. 'I will make it back, but maybe not on time,' he concedes.

The jaguar walks off. Zico stands rooted to the spot, more isolated than ever. The big cat paces in a small circle. With eyes locked on Zico, he strolls off again. This time, Zico interprets the gesture and follows.

They trek through the undergrowth with the jaguar cutting a path. After half an hour of solid walking, they stumble across the string. The forest now offers a partial view of the cliff and the village. Zico stops and strokes his guide. Suddenly, he realises he still has a job to complete.

'I've got to build a platform to jump from. Otherwise, I'll be stuck here forever.' Zico puffs out his chest. 'Courtesy of cable TV's Icy Adventures, I know how to cross the sandpit. I'll make snowshoes and use two sturdy sticks!'

Zico sets about constructing a platform, around one-and-a-half metres square. He cuts a dozen bamboo shoots, shaving off the leaves. Zico's eyes are drawn to the long thin tendrils from a creeper vine hanging from branches. *They will do nicely as twine.*

The jaguar watches on as Zico scurries up the tree. He cuts and drops the thinnest vines to the forest floor. The hollow jointed stems are tightly strung together. He twists the vines around them, two at a time, in a figure eight pattern. Zico uses the same technique to make snowshoes to help him glide-walk over the dunes.

He grabs his backpack and turns to the jaguar. 'I'll be back tomorrow unless it rains. I can't climb in the rain, it'll be way too slippery.' The jaguar's huge golden eyes blink. They have a chase and tumble before they part.

Zico emerges from the forest wearing bamboo shoes over his sneakers and carrying walking sticks. A length of vine secures the platform on his back. Then, like climbing stairs, Zico makes his way up the sandy surface. The further he goes, the deeper he sinks. Each footstep takes a toll on him.

He reaches the summit, totally exhausted. Untying his gear, he collapses to his knees to catch his breath. Zico sighs, 'There's got to be an easier way to get out of this place.'

The calmer he is, the more he is sucked into the pulverised sand. His idea was to use the base to stabilise the ground, but he is sinking fast. Zico fights to drag himself out of the pit. *The myth is no one who enters the forest ever returns.* He wonders, *is this the curse taking over now?*

After a huge effort, zapping almost all his energy, Zico scrambles on top of the platform. Carrying his weight, the structure begins to submerge.

Zico has only one chance to jump and grab the rope, or he will be swallowed up forever. The corner of the base closest to where he stands steadily sinks another half a metre. Zico clutches its top edge. He pulls his body in close to the platform before launching himself to his lifeline. Hands slipping and burning, he stubbornly holds on.

Zico dangles, kicking off the bamboo shoes. He uses the leverage of the rock to take the weight off him. After sucking in air and refocusing his efforts, he clambers up. With only ten metres to go, his determination grows.

As he climbs past the prison tower, he overhears a guard.

'Did you hear that, Julio?'

Hanging statue still with strength diminishing, Zico struggles to remain quiet. Worried the guards will shoot first and ask questions later, his palms pool with sweat. He hears a chair scraping, followed by heavy boots, and prays they don't do a wall-walk. The conversation from the tower is loud and clear.

'What noise?'

'Better take a look,' the guard says.

The door squeaks open. Feet pound the pavement.

'See anything?' the colleague asks.

'Nah. Something's off though. I can feel it.'

'Report it to the Capitan. We'll need to increase the patrols.'

The door clicks shut.

Zico's energy is burning out. He slides down a metre or so. Gritting his teeth, he musters all his strength. He has to get out of here. Clenching the rough rope in his aching hands, he climbs the final stretch. Zico drags himself over the rockface to safety and collapses on the ledge.

After a short while, he recovers enough to pull the rope up and hide it behind the boulder. Zico looks over the edge to the quicksand. The last visible section of the platform disappears in the crater's belly.

Sagging against the cliff as he catches his breath, Zico now understands the myth is not killing anyone. Whoever enters the forbidden zone drowns in the sand, just like he almost did. Except Zico came up with a plan to escape. And, being a lightweight helped.

Gazing into the forest he thinks, *the spirit of the jaguar is in me.*

CHAPTER 6

PAPER PLANES TO NOWHERE

C linging to the rock face, Zico surveys the hive of activity on the construction site. He is fearful his covert mission will fall under the scrutiny of Fonso and his crew. He zeros in on the foreman who shouts orders to the carpenters, who cascade instructions down to the labourers.

Zico is fascinated by the collaboration among the men. They're like a troop of Capuchin monkeys, sustained by cooperation, socialisation, and foraging for building materials and tools. It is mayhem.

Coming from the Amazon, and recently the Deep Forest, Zico realises this place is a different kind of jungle. It has its own laws. He needs to harness all his cunning to keep his adventure secret.

Timing is everything. His plan is to hide in plain sight. This requires moving at the same pace, seeing what they see, and reacting as they do. Studying the beat of the workers, Zico slinks over the wall.

Shuffling his feet as if there is nothing better to do, he sneaks a look around. His tongue lashes at the beads of sweat trickling down his face. It is now or never. Zico attempts to blend in, but his nerves take over. He picks up his stride and darts into the tent. Slumping to the floor, he lets out a sigh, heart beating like bongo drums.

He shrugs off his backpack, removes his filthy shirt, and switches it for a clean one. The magnitude of his accomplishment dawns on him. Zico silently celebrates, clenching his hands in victory fists. Searing pain causes him to wince. Uncurling his fingers, Zico is horrified by the sorry mess of ripped blisters spread across his palms.

He reaches for the backpack and pulls out the yellow ball. His face splits into a smirk. *Mission complete.*

★ ★ ★

Later that afternoon, munching on a banana at the railing, Zico wonders what the jaguar is up to. His thoughts are interrupted by a fast-moving object overhead.

The smooth movement of a shiny silver paper plane gliding across the landscape holds his attention. It crosses the border of Precious Above the Sea, passing directly over Fonso's house. Fascinated, Zico tracks the leisurely flight path. The glider soars and dips and steadies itself, before drifting over the Deep Forest. Zico follows every turn until it disappears into the canopy.

Moments later, an identical plane traces almost the same route. It swirls playfully until gravity takes hold, pulling it toward the earth.

Zico's eyes follow the plane's movement like a hawk seeking out prey. Just before the model enters the treetops, he is snapped back to the present by Fonso's bark.

'Zico!'

He turns around, shaken.

Fonso stares at him with jaws clamped shut and face flaming. Through gritted teeth, he growls, 'Is there something you want to tell me?'

Has Fonso cottoned on to my creative explanations? For Zico, honesty is a flexible thing. Squinting as if looking into the sun, a blush colours his cheeks. Zico is unable to hold Fonso's gaze.

Licking his lips, Zico consciously tenses and relaxes his muscles, waiting for what's to come. *Fonso warned me lies will result in conflict. How can he know about my adventure?* Zico takes a deep breath. His mind racing to find the right words to explain his disobedience.

Fonso explodes, 'Did someone cut you up? Who did this to you?' Firmly holding Zico's jaw, Fonso inspects his cheek.

'Ahh, the graze. I crashed into something.'

'What? Where? Here?'

Zico doesn't want to lie, but he cannot tell the truth. He points around wildly at everything, including the Deep Forest.

With eyes crinkled to slits, and a solemn shake of the head, Fonso probes. 'Again, is there something you want to tell me?'

Blinking back tears, Zico shakes himself loose from Fonso's grip and bows his head. He shoves his hands in his pockets, expels a heavy breath, and slowly looks up at his grandpa. He has learned if he stalls, Fonso's impatience will get the better of him. There is a fine line between truth and lies. He needs to handle this with care, otherwise, there will be consequences.

'What should I tell you?' Zico asks.

'The truth for a starter.'

Zico nods his head and takes a long breath. He headcounts, *one and two and three and...* delaying his confession of his mission to the Deep Forest.

By the time Zico counts five, Fonso changes tack. 'Your father just called me. He said earlier today he had a visit from the police. Does that trigger anything?'

Zico stares blankly. After the initial shock, he is baffled. 'No, why would a policeman see Dad? I don't understand.'

Fonso moves closer to him. 'From what your father told me, this is what happened...'

Back at the farm, a pollution spluttering moped passes through the gate and drives up to the house. It is confidently steered by a stern-faced Police Constable.

Zico's parents greet the surprise visitor at the front porch. They are all familiar with each other, having lived in the area for a long time. However, judging by his rigid posture and foreboding frown, this is not a friendly meeting.

The visit is about a fire that levelled the schoolhouse a while ago. A cap with Zico's name on it was found near where the investigators believe the inferno started.

The Constable asks many questions. Especially about Zico's attitude towards fires, his habits, and his recent state of mind. The word is, he bragged he lit the fire, so he didn't have to go to school. His mum and dad are worried about the claims. They agree Zico acts out, but doubt he would burn a building down on purpose.

Their assurance is brushed off like an annoying fly. Every day he listens to pleas of innocence from the relatives of criminals, even when they've been proven wrong. Zico's father withholds information about the blaze at Nothing Forever.

According to the policeman, forensics are investigating. The test on the petrol drenched cloth used to ignite the school should identify who the culprit is. He cautions Zico is in the frame of potential suspects.

Without further discussion, he mounts the moped and splutters down the driveway. Shell-shocked, Zico's parents retreat.

'That's when your father called me,' Fonso explains. He moves closer toward Zico's bruised face. 'Remember Zico, no lies. So, let's cut the nonsense. There are now three fires.'

1. *The fireplace in the courtyard where Fonso and Zico bond.*
2. *The house fire Zico attempted to extinguish.*
3. *The blaze that destroyed Zico's school.*

Fonso continues, 'Here's how I see it. One was accidental, one lit deliberately, and the other planned and started by someone else. Am I right?'

He leans forward with unblinking eye contact. 'Did you or did you not light the fire?'

'Which one are you talking about?'

Fonso almost gags on a cynical laugh. He rephrases, 'Are you responsible for the school arson?'

Zico shakes his head, 'No.' Sitting stone-still, but for biting his lip, Zico smoulders. Bitterly, he accuses, 'But my parents think I am!'

Fonso is quick to reassure him. 'Absolutely not.' He gives Zico a questioning look. 'They said the Constable told them you were bragging you did it.'

Zico protests, 'That's me getting attention.'

Fonso agrees. 'I believe you, and you know why? Because most crimes are claimed by people who never committed them. No difference here.'

Zico sighs his relief.

Fonso nods toward the house renovations. 'Have you seen the place?'

'No, not yet. I want to wait until it's done.'

'It won't take that much longer. They'll be finished tomorrow morning. Their last job is building a proper firepit here. What did you do all day?' Fonso asks.

'Exploring...'

Fonso grins, 'And running into things!'

Throwing his head back and letting out a loud laugh, Zico's eyes stream tears of relief. 'Yes.'

'Listen,' Fonso says. 'I searched for the ball this morning for a kick against the wall, but I couldn't find it. Where's your hiding spot?'

'Won't tell you!' Zico gets up, grabs the backpack from the tent, and produces the yellow ball. 'But during the day, the ball's in there.'

'Have you been in the real world today?' Fonso asks.

'Oh yes, and I want more of it! I'm thinking of going to the colosseum later, but first I need some food.' Zico says.

'Plenty over there,' Fonso points to the table. 'I'll arrange a feast for us tonight. Last night out in the wild, Zico.'

Fonso strolls over to the house. Slapping the builders on the back, it is clear he is happy with the developments. He issues a few instructions before disappearing through the gate.

Zico settles at the table and helps himself to the food. He wonders, *how on earth will I return to the Deep Forest without dying in the sandpit* . Two tradies join him. They unbuckle their tool belts and drop them with a heavy clunk and clatter, right next to Zico's plate.

The hustle of activity provides a perfect cover for Zico to acquire tools for his secret operation. *The hooks on the belts could come in handy. I could secure the rope to the rock wall, and use them to attach a second line. Then, span the extension over the most dangerous section of the sand.*

Zico identifies items vital for this plan: two hooks from the work belt, a rope as long as possible, paint to match the rope's colour to the sand, and a brush or cloth.

Inching his hand forward, Zico pauses and drums his fingers. He talks about nothing in general with the builders, who respond with an occasional grunt. Inch by inch, he moves closer to the prize.

As Zico caresses the smooth metal of the hooks, a meaty hand slams down on his wrist.

'Oi. What are you up to?' the carpenter shouts.

'Me?' Sweat beads on Zico's forehead. 'I was just looking.'

'Looking to swipe something, more like it.'

Eyes drilling into Zico, the plumber butts in. 'Miguel and Bernardo were arguing earlier about missing tools. What do you know about that?'

Shaking his head desperately, Zico pleads, 'N, no, nothing.'

The men stand over him. They are menacing.

Composing himself, Zico attempts to outwit them. 'From what I understand, possession is a temporary thing here.' He waves his hand at the worksite. 'Anyone could be responsible.'

The plumber gobs spit that lands millimetres from Zico's feet. He stares hard at Zico. 'I'm watching you!'

They grab their tool belts and head back to work, exchanging insults about the kid.

Zico is upset with himself. He had a chance to snatch the hooks but was too slow to act. He fumes as he watches the tradies walking away. With their whinging and moaning, word is sure to get out.

Sinking his head in his hands he thinks, *my plans are ruined!* Zico moves to the ledge and peers down at the forest, eyes misting with angry tears. He feels the jaguar calling him. *His spirit is in me – that means I have courage! I can't give up now.*

I'll need to be crafty. Zico surveys the worksite to see what else can be of use. No ropes can be seen, but there is plenty of paint. He pulls out his notebook.

Plan A – Don't get caught. Blend in, and get out fast!
Plan B – Don't confess. I'm helping clean up the site.

Edging towards the tins, he casts a sly glance around. Zico stretches his arms out, rotating them a few times in circles. On the next forward swing, he hooks a tin in each hand, then hurries to the bathroom. Using empty buckets, Zico mixes colours: dark grey for the cliff, and light beige for the quicksand. Job done.

He seals the containers airtight and returns them to where he found them. He snatches a broomstick. Scurrying off, he stores his loot in his hiding place.

★ ★ ★

Late afternoon, Zico straps on his backpack and scans the tent. He makes sure everything is put away. A toothy grin spreads across his face. He has been looking forward to immersing himself in the electrifying atmosphere of the colosseum. He is a fast learner. Once he discovers a place, he is a human GPS. All the same, he stuffs Fonso's map in his pocket, just in case.

Leaping into action, with feet hammering the pavement, he races through the hillside village. As he sprints down the last few steps, the buzz of the crowd courses through him. Springing up and down on the balls of his feet, he seeks out a better vantage point.

Zico manoeuvres through the mob, heading for the crates on the far side. He spots the kid who took the ball from him. Ducking, he sidesteps, trying to get out of his line of sight. It's too late. The thief zeroes in on him.

Without thinking, Zico pivots on his heels and takes off, shoving people out of his way. Head down, arms and legs pumping, Zico just wants to escape.

He realises from the jeers and shouts behind him that his foe is in hot pursuit. They run up and down stairs, and through narrow passages. A quick glance over his shoulder tells him the odds are stacked against him. Turning a corner, Zico is trapped. It's a dead end.

Mind whirling, Zico strategises how he can talk himself out of a bashing. This kid is much bigger and stronger, and for some reason, he has targeted him. He pushes up his sleeves as he approaches the helpless Zico.

The thief winds up his arm and pounds him in the face. Blood spurts from Zico's nose as he falls to the ground.

'You think you're something special because you're the Patrão's grandson. You're nothing to us, dweeb. You don't belong here jungle boy!'

Zico peers up at the menacing boy. He wipes the blood away with the back of his hand, and leans against the wall. *If I don't get up, I'm a wimp, if I do, I'll probably be knocked down again.* Pride bigger than ego, Zico hauls himself up. Heart galloping, he takes a few rasping breaths, ready to face his attacker.

Zico's voice shakes, 'I guess from where you kicked the ball, you saw where it went.'

The kid sneers, and with a flourish he gestures a long dive. 'Into the Deep Forest. Gone, what a shame. A reliable source told me it is a one-of-a-kind ball.' His lips curl in contempt.

Zico shrugs off his backpack, unsnaps the clasps, and produces the yellow ball. All the time, his confidence growing. His pursuer inhales sharply. He is stunned to silence. Zico playfully flicks the ball from one hand to the other. Then, wiggling his fingers in front of his tormentor's face, Zico mimics a ghost, 'Booo.'

Contempt morphs into horror. 'The spirits are in you!' Stumbling backward, the kid spins and runs, slipping several times on his retreat. Zico returns the ball to his bag. He whoops with laughter as he cruises back to the colosseum, his body battered, but his spirit soaring.

By now the press of the crowd is claustrophobic. They jostle Zico like a pinball, until he thumps into a container wall. Zico scrambles to stay on his feet. He hoists himself up the pipes to safety. Not only is he elevated to a premium position, but without knowing, he plonks himself in the coach's box.

Zico witnesses a heated game. It is an entertaining contest. The ball rockets through the net, punches are thrown, and the referee issues a yellow card. Zico wants to establish how skilled these teams really are. He sidles up to the coach. 'It's an exciting match, you must be happy?'

The man in charge is Alberto Sultras. He is a beer-drinking, sloppy and unshaven character who appears twenty years older than he actually is. 'As pleased as you can get for a loser team.'

Zico squints up at him. 'But you're winning.'

'Exactly,' Sultras confirms.

Sultras picks up on Zico's confusion. He chuckles, 'You're the Patrão's boy, right?'

'Yes. My name's Zico.'

'Welcome to the real world, Zico. I knew your father when he was little. You look like him; he always came out second best in scuffles too,' he laughs. 'I guess you're not here for a history lesson. You want to know how this is a losing team, right?'

Zico nods vigorously.

'These two teams are in the losers' comp. There is also a winners' comp. Needless to say, they are better outfits. This fixture is made up of leftovers. I like misfits, they are unpredictable and a lot more fun.' He pauses for breath. 'At the end of the season, the best losers' team plays the worst winners' team for relegation. The best losers' winning team just happens to be my squad.'

'So, your winners are losers,' Zico summarises.

Sultras nods, distracted by one of his players being badly fouled.

For the remainder of the game, Sultras' bunch continues with a man down, and they win by one goal. Sultras grabs Zico on his way out. 'You play?' he asks.

Zico is unsure how to answer him. 'Not at that level.'

Offended, Sultras shoots back, 'What? You're too special for this comp?'

Zico backtracks clumsily, 'No, no, actually I'm an average player. I'm better with my hands than my feet.'

Sultras declares, 'Perfect. You'll be the goalie then.'

Lost for words but recognising a response is expected, Zico asks, 'So, what's this team called?'

'White Shirts! You're in?'

Wide-eyed, Zico stutters, 'Y, ye, yes.'

Sultras asks, 'Do you want to meet your new teammates now?'

Zico shakes his head, 'Nah, see you tomorrow.' He hurdles the barricade to exit the colosseum for the second time that day.

Sultras yells after him, 'See you at seven. It's an evening fixture against the Hillimancharoes. Don't be late and wear a white shirt.'

★ ★ ★

The sky is clear and the night is calm. Fonso is roasting the food over the fireplace. Zico yawns endlessly. His bones are aching and his head is buzzing with excitement. Sadly, he acknowledges he cannot share most of it with anyone.

I've been to the Deep Forest. Recovered my ball. Made friends with a wild jaguar. I stood-up to the kid who stole from me. Joined a football team. And, I haven't lied about anything. What an achievement! Zico smiles. *This is what I'd like to say in answer to Fonso when he asks, 'How was your day, Zico?'*

'Zico. Zico!' Fonso's firm voice shakes him from his thoughts. 'Are the kids giving you trouble? Do you need me to step in?'

'Ah, you mean my nose,' Zico lightly pinches his nostrils. It is swollen and tender. 'It's nothing. We were running. Then I fell down.'

'Making friends, eh? It looks like you ran into someone's fist!' Fonso fixes his eyes on his grandson, in search of answers.

Zico side-steps Fonso's fact-finding mission. 'The best part of the day was meeting Sultras. You won't believe what happened!'

Fonso is curious about Zico's football career which is set to take off the next day. 'The White Shirts are a really good bad team. Their coach is a friend of mine.

It's great you'll be their goalie! What are your skills like?'

'We'll find out tomorrow,' Zico stifles a yawn.

'Why don't I give you a bit of a warm-up here at 5 o'clock, before we go to the game?'

Zico does a double-take, 'You're coming?'

'Sure. Wouldn't miss it,' Fonso winks.

'They're on top of their comp!'

'Yes,' nods Fonso, 'but more importantly, the White Shirts play fair, unlike most of the others. See, they put their values and principles above their interests.'

'What does that mean?' Zico interrupts.

'A value is what you're made of, things that encourage meaning to you and shape your character. Principle is how you behave when implementing your values. Say the team wants to win every game — this is an example of interest. The values are to treat players fairly and make sure the squad sticks to this behaviour out of principle.'

Zico stares at Fonso. 'Huh?'

'In other words, they won't win at all costs. 'All costs' means they throw out their team values and principles and start cheating or playing foul. The White Shirts don't do that. Their coach will tell you that before he throws you into the fray,' Fonso explains.

Zico nods sluggishly. The lids on his heavy eyes drop, closing out an eventful day. Fonso spreads a blanket over Zico, pleased that his grandson is finally having an adventure.

CHAPTER 7

PRECIOUS DISCOVERY

T he next morning, Zico experiences a dull and persistent ache in his bones as he strolls around the courtyard. The army of workers has shrunk. It is down to three painters, two carpenters, an electrician, and a technician tuning a weird looking box.

Zico spots a laptop on the table. He checks the coast is clear and settles in front of it. Fingers race across the keyboard, making the pitter-patter sound of gentle rain.

He searches for equipment to help climb in and out of the forest. Clicking through adventure sport websites, Zico works out the type of gear he really needs. *This sucks! For the first time ever, I've got money to spend but I can't buy a thing.* Without a credit card, the online shop is closed.

He assesses his blistered hands, squeezing and releasing them several times. *Using tools not fit for purpose increases the risk with each climb.*

From the corner of his eye, Zico is alerted to the technician's focus shifting toward him. He clears his search and slides his butt along the bench.

At the end of the table are a neatly folded white t-shirt and goalie gloves. Zico's heart swells. *Today is going to be a good day.* He sits, smiling in a silly way before pushing himself up. Back to business.

Zico walks by the carpenters mixing concrete to pour the foundation for the new outdoor firepit. He greets them with a brief smile. Pulling the binoculars from his pocket, he moves to the edge of the courtyard. He is desperate to locate the jaguar in the Deep Forest. He scratches his head. *Where is he?* Bending over the ledge, he stares down at the quicksand and murmurs, 'Here we go again.'

He brushes his teeth, throws on fresh clothes, and packs the ball and water bottle into his backpack. He peels a banana, scoffing it down, intent to start his expedition as soon as possible.

The tent blocks the tradies' view of Zico's cliffside route into the forest. He tucks the broomstick under his belt, checking it is secure.

Then he slides down the rope and passes the prison tower.

Dangling just above the crater, Zico flings the backpack to the sand, then swings on it. He sand-surfs down the slope. With the wind whipping his face, Zico's adrenaline pumps. This time he is more skilful. Using the broomstick for balance he bends his knees, digging his heels in to slow the ride.

At the bottom, Zico dusts himself off. He makes his way into the woods, the string guiding his path. Heart racing, he searches for the jaguar. No luck! Zico follows the thread deeper into the forest. Bewildered, he spins around, seeking signs of movement. Engulfed with loss, he concedes the animal was a fabrication of his imagination.

The overwhelming hush of grief is shattered. With four gigantic bounds, the playful cat pounces on Zico, knocking him over.

Startled by the ambush, Zico shrieks, 'You got me!'

The jaguar releases a loud rumble as he nudges Zico with his nose and licks his face.

He invites Zico to follow him. They stray off the path into the thicket. Zico is vigilant but curious, and he trusts his new friend. The jaguar stops at a magnificent towering tree. He curls his body around the base and rubs his head into it, purring. Zico copies him, wrapping his arms around the trunk. He declares, 'I Zico, defender of the free spirit, name you the Tree of Love.'

The jaguar pokes Zico on and then lunges ahead. Glancing back occasionally, he leads Zico through the bush into a hidden opening. The filtered light is almost magical. This bay, fifty metres across, sheltered by treetops and concealed from the outside world, is the jaguar's home. The tranquil emerald green waterway is surrounded by lush trees.

It is the most beautiful place Zico has ever seen. The bay is abundant with vibrant vegetation and wildlife. He flops to the ground. Lying on his belly, resting his chin in his hands, he takes it all in. Searching his mind for a suitable word to describe it, *pristine* rolls off his tongue. He never used the descriptor before but thinks it fits.

This place is a million miles away from the scrap yard that is Nothing Forever. Zico marvels at the butterflies dancing dizzily above his head. He observes the brilliant flashy feathers of parrots flying to the safety of a higher perch. After a while, he plays ball with the jaguar. They splash and swim in the bay.

Zico wonders about the salty water. *There must be an underwater opening to the ocean.*

Ever the surveyor, he checks the sun's position. He explains to the jaguar, 'I need to go back now. Rain is predicted tomorrow, so I'll come again in two days.' Before leaving, Zico declares, 'I Zico, protector of sacred places, name this the Bay of Plenty.'

The jaguar nods his agreement and they stroll off.

On their way back, Zico discovers a stack of paper planes, twelve in total, in a small cave. He is impressed by the level of care and protection the remarkable animal gives them.

Zico is eager to share his own experience of the planes. 'I watch them every day gliding over my house. You really look after them!'

The jaguar is pleased.

'May I?'

The jaguar bows. Zico inspects the intricate aerodynamic gliders and their precise design. He opens his notebook and sketches the plane, recording its blueprint. They are numbered at the back with neat handwriting and signed by 'Sancia'.

The jaguar nudges the aircraft that Zico holds.

Zico pulls his arm back into launch position. 'You want me to throw one?'

The jaguar shakes his head. He gently knocks the plane from Zico's hand, nuzzling the centre of it delicately. He gazes up at Zico with blinking eyes.

Zico looks closer at the aircraft and realises it carries a message on the inside. He opens the folds and reads:

I am an object collected by my parents. Packaged in a pretty pink bow, to be looked at and not played with. Their perfect world is my worst nightmare. Sancia.

Zico unfolds one plane after another and reads the text to his friend. The more he recites the more he is intrigued by the content.

'I really want to meet Sancia. She is very good with words. I could never express my feelings this way,' Zico confides. He jots down keywords from the messages next to his drawings of the planes.

Perfect world
Not coping
Indulgence gone crazy
Perfection undone
Foolish me
Owning an adventure
Company of one
Knowledge is power
Opinions count

Dare to try
Vertical disparity
Immense waste

A short while later, Zico cuddles the jaguar goodbye. He departs the Deep Forest much faster. Wearing a new set of snowshoes to scale the sandy crater, Zico carries a freshly tied bamboo base underarm.

His first jump from the platform to the rope is a miss. He crashes on the sinking raft. Preparing to launch again, Zico knows it is going to be his last shot at it. Stretching his arms to capacity, Zico grabs hold of the rope as high as possible. He steadies himself by pinching the rope between his feet, then pulls his way to the top.

Zico realises his escape out of this treacherous crater is based more on luck than skill.

Whilst not physically challenging, returning from the cliff's edge to the courtyard unnoticed, requires stealth. It is the part of the adventure that makes him most nervous. Zico is all too aware Fonso has eyes and ears everywhere. He is determined not to be found out.

Poking his head over the wall, he scans the area for worker activity. To his surprise, no one is there.

The natural rock firepit is finished. All the tools are gone. The site is tidy and eerily quiet. He drops his backpack on the courtyard's pebbled stone floor. Then, spreading his arms into wings, Zico pretends to glide into the house. He stops dead-still at the door.

The interior is of high quality, sparkly and new. He is pleased the bunk-robe now has a glass barricade to protect him from the steep drop. Zico tippy-toes across the polished wooden floorboards, not wanting to muck them up with his grubby footprints.

The open kitchen is tiled in deep green. The fridge is double in size. All cupboards and utensils are clean and functional. The shower is gone, making space for a much bigger flat-screen TV. The receiver box is connected to the screen and the lead vanishes into the wall socket.

Zico walks outside with a cola in hand. He is certain this is the most stylish house ever.

He sits by the firepit, trying to work out how to spark it to life without any wood. His focus is distracted by a movement in the sky. He follows the out-of-control flight of a paper plane. The aircraft spirals in a nosedive. It wedges itself in a wooden panel of the fence separating Nothing Forever from Precious Above the Sea.

Zico murmurs, 'Unlucky thirteen. I wonder what Sancia is up to today.'

He plots a pathway up the rock wall to retrieve the crashed plane. The route ascends the fifteen-metre vertical cliff and leads to a narrow ledge. When he reaches the top, all he needs to do is climb the massive fence and snatch the plane.

It can't be any worse than climbing in and out of the Deep Forest. Always the strategist, he plans for unforeseen eventualities. *If I get caught, I might need to pay someone off. If I fall, I'll need money for a doctor. If I'm lucky, someone will be selling ice-cream behind the wall!* He grabs his cash from his stash and stuffs it in his sock.

Scaling the rock, he realises how easy it would be for anyone up there to come down here. Fonso's voice echoes in his head. *Up there are the people within the flag; we can't see them, and they definitely don't want to see us, meet us, or talk to us.*

Zico reaches up and touches the two-and-a-half-metre solid fence, dividing the two cultures. He is high up with nowhere to go but down. The ledge is tiny, but there is room enough for him to stand.

He climbs up the planks with ease, getting closer to the stricken paper plane. Zico grabs the glider and starts to climb down. *I've lost my marbles! I'm not going to waste this opportunity.* His curiosity urges him to peek into the Precious Above the Sea world.

Gripping the top of the barrier with both hands, Zico swings his hips to build momentum. He hoists himself up until his chin rests on the ridge of the wall. With his biceps burning, Zico's feet scramble up the structure, reducing the strain on his upper body.

The view blows his mind. Especially, when only ten minutes ago, he thought nothing could ever exceed the interior of Fonso's house. *What a rich world!*

One of the modern, gleaming glass high-rise towers spirals like a staircase and has a pool on each balcony. Tennis courts, pools, and an outdoor gym are dotted between himself and the incredible buildings.

A girl's firm voice startles him. 'Jump over the fence and drop my plane.'

Zico pulls himself higher to see who is talking to him.

She is the most beautiful girl ever. Curly golden-brown hair, green eyes, and light honey coloured skin. She wears clothes you only see in the movies. Her confident wave of a mobile phone completes her style. Zico believes she must be twelve but looks fourteen and acts sixteen!

When she repeats the order, she is blunt. 'I said, jump over the fence and drop my plane. Otherwise, I'll call the guards, and they will shoot you.'

The last bit snaps Zico back to reality. 'You can't be serious, that's mad.'

The girl turns around to check if anyone is close by. She waves her phone at him like a sword, ready to speed dial for help. Zico swings his body up and over the fence. The high-pitched warbling of the security siren is activated, its scream shaking the air.

Both he and the girl are startled into statues. No time to spare; they take off in a reckless run. She thinks she will be in trouble. Zico knows he is in over his head.

'Come, quick.' She pushes him into a shed at the tennis courts, slams the door shut, and locks it. Inside is pitch-black.

Through the gaps between the wooden slats, Zico can see armed security swarming the place. They challenge her, 'What happened? Did someone cross the border?'

'No, no one came over. There was a black cat roaming around the wall a minute ago,' she answers.

Zico is impressed by her confidence. She is good. The guards relax. After checking the grounds, they reset the alarm and move back to their positions.

Sancia unlocks and opens the door a fraction. 'The plane, now,' she says.

Zico immediately gives in to her demand.

She blatantly inspects him from head to toe. After a long silence, she wedges the door open. 'Come with me. If anyone asks, you're my cousin. Let's go.'

Zico follows her. In the elevator, she studies him as she explains the fault with the plane's flight path. He is mesmerised. This is the first time in his life to ride an elevator. Zico is so excited he finds it difficult to keep up with the girl as she prattles on.

'So, I decided to launch the plane from a different point, which I'll never do again! I'm careful with my planes. From construction to flight conditions, I work everything out. All my other launches glided safely to their destination in the Deep Forest.'

The level six penthouse is magnificent with floor-to-ceiling windows, framing nature's masterpiece. She keeps a watchful eye on Zico. People always gush and compliment her parents on their style, but she's never witnessed such a reaction. It is confronting. He is obviously awed by the pool on the terrace. Taking in the abundance of the villa, Zico's face broadcasts a mixture of desire and shame.

She is intrigued by him. 'What's your name?'

'Zico,' he says without looking at her. Spinning in slow motion, he struggles to comprehend the luxury that she lives in.

'I'm Sancia. You're from Nothing Forever, uh?'

'Not really. I'm on holiday there,' he answers.

Her laugh is full of sarcasm. 'On vacation in one of the most neglected parts of the country. Where are you from?'

'A cacao farm in Tocantins.'

'A poor jungle boy,' Sancia says.

'Don't call me poor or jungle boy. I may not live rich like you, but at least I don't have poor manners! Do you need to see my money to see my worth?'

From his sock, Zico pulls out 500 Reais and shakes it in her face.

Surprised, Sancia backtracks. 'Sorry Zico, I didn't mean to offend. It's just, like, I'm normally not around...'

With eyes flashing, Zico cuts in. 'People like me.'

Sancia agrees, 'Yes.'

After an awkward silence, Sancia asks, 'What made you climb up the rock face? Was it just to retrieve the plane?'

Zico shrugs, 'Something to do, I guess.'

'You could fall. That's a massive risk to take.'

'With risk there's reward. Well, I'm here now, meeting you.' He relaxes a bit. 'Why didn't you turn me in?'

Sancia smiles. 'As you say, every risk has its rewards. I think it will be more fun with you around.'

Zico follows her as she moves through the rooms like an animated dancer.

'You have no idea how badly I'm in trouble.' They pass an office with a 3D model displayed in the centre of the room. 'I'm grounded here for my holidays. It's the worst punishment. Can you believe it?' She stops and stares at Zico, waiting for a reaction.

Zico is baffled, 'No, I can't.'

Sancia continues, 'Instead of a skiing vacation in Switzerland, I'm stuck here. What a disaster! If they see me with you — you know we should never mix — all hell will break loose. I'm already considered to be the odd-one-out in Precious Above the Sea.'

'I know how that is, Sancia. Except rather than enjoying a holiday in Europe, I ended up at...' he stops himself, ashamed.

'Nothing Forever,' she completes.

Zico nods, 'It's an interesting place. The bonus is, the Deep Forest is on its doorstep.'

Sancia rolls her eyes, 'Really?'

'Really,' Zico responds.

Sancia accuses, 'It sounds like you're saying you've been to the Deep Forest.'

'Yes, I went down there,' Zico admits.

'I don't believe you!'

'I have,' he implores.

'No, you haven't. Otherwise, you would not be here. The forest would swallow you up.' Sancia imitates a spooky ghost, 'Or perhaps it already has, and you are a spirit.'

Zico turns away angrily. 'Whatever!' Wanting to impress her, he boasts, 'I've even met the jaguar that roams around down there.'

'You met a jaguar on your expedition to the forest?' Sancia suspects Zico is lying. She teases, 'Okay, prove it?'

He approaches her desk to take a closer look at the production line of paper planes. They face the clean glass window, overlooking the Deep Forest and the distant ocean. The stack of silver metallic A4 paper and some partially folded gliders indicate perfection at work. Five planes are completed and are sequentially numbered below their left-wing from 14 to 19.

Sancia invites Zico to play truth or dare to get to the bottom of his claims. She insists she will ask him a question that he must answer truthfully. If not, Zico must perform a dare from a selection of three propositions. Zico demands that if he answers honestly, it is Sancia who must carry out a dare. After some calculated deliberation, both shake hands in a business-like agreement.

Zico asks, 'So what do you want to know?'

Sancia stares at Zico defiantly. 'Did you really go to the Deep Forest?'

Zico says, 'Yes. A couple of times.'

'You're lying,' she hisses.

'I have been there,' Zico states, this time with more force.

'Prove it. You can't! I win. End of story,' she responds.

Zico counters, 'I'm here, I made it back.'

Sancia's laugh is loaded with cynicism, 'You are a fraudster.'

A sudden moment of brilliance establishes another angle which he thinks will prove his claim. Zico is pumped. 'Your paper planes are numbered, and you fly them in sequence,' he says in an assured voice.

She is shocked and almost gives in until she remembers Zico looking at her workstation earlier. 'You saw my production line.' Without hesitation, she triumphantly thinks out loud, 'Okay, now to your deeds. Let me think about what you should do.'

Zico interrupts, 'Your planes carry messages — very personal messages.'

Sancia's jaw drops and she gasps in disbelief. 'One of the planes must've crashed.'

'No crash, no interception. You said earlier they all went into the forest. You never flew one without checking the weather, and never in the rain,' Zico smirks.

'Not proof enough,' she retorts.

'Give me a number from one to twelve,' Zico insists.

Sancia launched thirteen planes. He could only know them if he read them down at the Deep Forest. Pale-faced she almost whispers, 'Six.'

'Six!' Zico confirms.

To her astonishment, Zico pulls out a notepad. She waits anxiously as he flicks through the pages.

'Plane six's message was about, uh, owning an adventure.'

Sancia concedes, 'You have been there! Tell me about it.' Anger overrides awe as realisation hits: he is aware of her most personal thoughts. She accuses, 'You read them and made notes about my private feelings. How dare you!' Sancia slaps at his face.

Zico jumps back. 'Are you crazy? You wanted the truth, you don't like it, and now you're hitting me.'

Sancia is shocked by her behaviour. 'I'm so sorry, Zico. I have never hit someone before. I'm sorry.' Disappointed with herself, she asks him to leave.

'Just like that?'

Sancia nods tearfully.

'I will never tell anybody your stuff. Uh, actually, I already did,' Zico confesses.

Crest-fallen Sancia wails, 'Who? Who did you tell?'

Zico grins sheepishly. 'The jaguar.'

'You read my messages to a mammal?' She shakes her head dismissively. 'It seems like you have a wild imagination.'

Zico defends himself. 'No, not at all. Listen, I've got to go. I need to get ready to play football in the colosseum.'

Hesitantly she says, 'A deal's a deal. What deed do you want me to do?'

'Just help me find a way out of here without being shot,' Zico half-jokes.

She agrees, grabs a second mobile phone, and leads him down to the forecourt and across to the fence. Sancia points to a bush. She shows him a gap in the border, heading towards the roof of the prison tower.

Before Zico disappears, Sancia hands him the device. 'This is my spare phone. It's yours now. I'll text you tomorrow. Hey, make sure you message the right number. There are only two numbers saved other than mine — my parents. They certainly won't want to hear from you!'

Surprised, Zico takes the phone. He asks, 'Why?'

'I want to know how your match goes. Text me the outcome,' she smiles.

Zico looks up at her and grins. 'Nice to meet you, Sancia.' He pushes his way into the bush and slips through the breach in the fence.

CHAPTER 8

THE CALM BEFORE THE STORM

Zico enters the house. He is surprised to find Fonso playing with the TV's remote control.

Fonso asks, 'Where were you?'

'Exploring the neighbourhood.' Zico drops his head, uncomfortable with his deception.

Fonso's attention is on the flat-screen and not Zico. 'What do you think?'

'You mean the goalie gloves and white T-shirt? Or the football goal you got for us?' Zico asks.

'Uh, yeah, that as well,' Fonso responds.

'It's great. I can practice before the match.' Zico swings open the fridge and swigs milk from the bottle. 'What else did I miss?'

Fonso turns to Zico and nods toward the television. 'We've got the Ferrari of all cable TV connections. Courtesy of an Indian communications satellite, not to mention the ingenuity of a tech guy. He tapped into a satellite 60 to 70 degrees west of Greenwich. We've now got the best Brazilian service! This is a bit unauthorised but worth over 220 channels.'

'220! You'll never need to leave the house.'

'Just don't burn it down,' Fonso jokes. 'You know, tonight we should pack up the tent. A storm's forecast for tomorrow.'

Fonso continues to play with his new toy. Zico slouches on his bunk. He is disappointed camping has come to an end. Removing Sancia's mobile phone from his pocket, Zico activates silent mode. He checks the battery — charged at 96% — and hides the device under the cushions.

The sun is behind the Precious Above the Sea buildings, drawing long shadows over the courtyard. They drag the tent closer to the house, making room for the football practice session. A goal is set up against the cliff face. Zico wears his new white t-shirt, black shorts, and sneakers.

'I won't kick the ball too hard, just in case I miss the goal. I don't want to lose it to the Deep Forest,' Fonso says. He boots the ball at Zico for him to save.

Zico's hand-eye coordination is solid but that doesn't mean he is ready for the hothouse. The other teams apply all kinds of tricks; they use methods that may not be in line with the official rules.

The intense goalkeeping training session forces Zico to step up. He practices mid-level dives, fisting balls, and parrying shots. Only a few times, Fonso's pace and accuracy beat him for goal.

Session over, Fonso grabs the ball and high-fives Zico. 'I reckon you are the only Brazilian who's happy to be a goalkeeper,' he says.

Zico laughs it off. 'I'm in a team, an actual football team, without having any ball skills.'

'Hey, what are talking about,' Fonso interjects. 'I struggled to score.' He slings his arm around Zico's shoulders. 'Have fun tonight. The colosseum can be intimidating. Take a deep breath and stay within the moment. Before you know it, the game will be over.'

The hillside village is blanketed by darkness. Zico and Fonso are coaxed along the path by the chaotic cheers coming from the colosseum. As they make their way closer, the pitch-black of the night is interrupted by stark shadows. Fluorescent globes hanging over every front door filter light across the stairs.

Zico's heart races and his body tingles with excitement. *This entrance is like walking down an alley of stars.* He basks in the glory.

His daydream is broken by a rush of people pushing past to greet their Patrão. Zico witnesses first-hand how much his grandpa is adored by the community. His chest swells with pride. *No matter what happens on the pitch, this is a night I'll always remember.*

The colosseum is packed. Every possible light source is deployed to illuminate the playing area. Fonso takes his seat in the VIP box: a large balcony at someone's home. On the field, Sultras introduces Zico to his teammates.

The referee conducts the hothouse like an orchestra. Holding his whistle aloft, he silences the crowd. Then, almost in slow motion, he places the instrument in his mouth. With all eyes trained on him, he inhales and blows a long, shrill sound. The audience erupts. Game on.

Zico takes a deep breath, steadying himself for battle. Five a side, the White Shirts face the Hillimancharoes. They are a formidable-looking outfit dressed all in black. The mind games, skills, and sheer force are evenly balanced. Zico makes several incredible saves and concedes two goals whilst the White Shirts score three times. At half time, Zico scans the spectators for Fonso. When their eyes meet, Fonso gives him a double thumbs up.

The second half is more physical than the first. Positioned off the goal line, hands up and bouncing, Zico zeros in on his opponent. He waits for the rocket that is about to be launched.

The boy is a steamroller intent on demolishing the net. Three of Zico's teammates are swatted away like flies as they attempt to take the ball. The fourth tracks him at a safe range. Nothing is slowing this massive kid down. It is a one-on-one standoff now, and he is within spitting distance of Zico. The steamroller pulls back his right leg before whipping it forward. Zico blocks the ball and the player who propels him backward, smashing him to the ground.

Bruised and battered, Zico lies still. He flexes his muscles to make sure everything is still attached. His hand sears with pain. Rapidly blinking, he attempts to clear the stars in his eyes.

The steamroller stands over him. 'You were frozen in fear!'

Zico brushes off the jibe. He counters, 'Nah, you were never getting it through.'

Pulling himself up, he plays down the injury and goes on as if nothing happened. The minutes fly by and the referee's whistle blasts the end of the match.

They win by three goals, eight-five. The crowd lets out a loud cheer. Zico shakes hands with the players. Then his new friends form a circle around him, marking their victory with a samba dance. Celebrations are kept short. The next teams are on the pitch, waiting for the blast of the whistle.

Sultras ushers the White Shirts out of the colosseum. 'If we win the next game, we qualify for the play-offs against the wooden-spooners from the winners' comp.

On a high, one of the teammates sings, 'We're winners. We're winners.'

Before the tune becomes a chant, Sultras cuts him off. 'Just because they're coming last doesn't mean we've got it in the bag. Everyone's pride is at stake. If they lose, they'll be relegated and, if that happens, we'll be promoted.'

★ ★ ★

In the sanctuary of Fonso's compound, Zico's hand is packed in ice. He relives his greatest sporting achievements, while Fonso breaks down the tent.

'I'm so proud of you. The last time a family member competed in the colosseum was two decades ago,' Fonso beams.

Zico's excitement is overflowing. 'The game was amazing. And, tomorrow we play for the relegation spot!'

Fonso shows Zico some images he took on his mobile. As he swipes through the photos, one action shot stands out.

'Go back, look at that! How did I do that? Can you text it to me? He was a beast. Did you see how I stood my ground?'

'You have a phone?' Fonso queries, surprised.

'Nah, not really. Just borrowed it while I'm here,' Zico answers.

Fonso's brows raise in a sceptical shrug. He eyes Zico curiously.

Zico thinks, *the line between truth and lies is becoming murky* . He decides the best way forward is another partial truth. 'I don't even know the number. That's how insignificant this phone is to me.'

'Get it and call me,' Fonso insists.

Zico retrieves the phone. As Fonso recites his number, Zico dials. Fonso disconnects the call, storing the details under *Zico* . His thick index finger thumps the keypad surprisingly fast. A second later,

Zico's phone lights up. He opens the text to see his favourite photo, captioned as *colossal save* . With a grin splitting his face, Zico stares at the image. *What a sweet moment.* He saves the private number as *Fonso*.

Lightning strikes the Deep Forest. It is followed by an enormous rumble of thunder. 'Let's get inside, quick,' Fonso commands.

They rush to collect the dismantled tent. Running into the house, they shove the gear in the cupboard. Apart from their soggy appearance, the place is spic and span.

'I guess we cook in here tonight,' Fonso says. He checks what is in the fridge.

Zico reflects on the busiest day of his life. From his bunk window, he stares into the forest, worrying about the jaguar's wellbeing.

He picks up the mobile phone then drops it like a hot potato. Zico chuckles softly. He thinks, *I can single-handedly stop a steamroller, but I'm scared of texting a girl.*

Staring at the phone he works up the courage to activate the screen. He accesses the contacts and searches Sancia's number. Then he adds the photo of him parrying the shot. Zico keys in the message: *We won 8:5. Have a great night. Zico.* He reads the text several times. Pressing send generates a huge smile.

Fonso grabs a few items and places them on the table. 'This fridge doesn't make sense, yet. We'll eat a simple dinner. We've got bread and spreads. Help yourself.' Then he jokes, 'Otherwise the five-star restaurant is one level up.'

As with every night so far, once they sit down, Zico tells Fonso about his day. Lying is avoided. He divulges he explored, discovered, and has been busier than ever.

After seeing what Fonso means to the community, Zico has more respect for him. He wonders, *is now the time to tell him everything?*

Fonso asks, 'Have you called your parents yet?'

Zico shakes his head. 'No, I want them to miss me a bit more.'

'You got their number?' Fonso probes.

Zico drops his head, frustrated and embarrassed. Reaching across the table, Fonso raises Zico's chin. He takes some time searching his grandson's glazed eyes.

'How do you think I achieved respect from these people?' he asks.

Zico shrugs and mumbles, 'I don't know.'

'In the beginning, by force. Kind of still is but in a much more refined way. This organised chaos works because I am perceptive. The people here need strong leadership. The common-sense approach you get from a gut feeling. Now, my gut tells me you live in your own world and, I believe you don't lie. However, you don't tell the whole truth.' Fonso takes a huge bite of bread.

Zico recognises he met his match with Fonso, but unlike his parents, Fonso encourages two-way communication. His mind spins, trying to work out which half-truths Fonso detected and what gave them away.

He takes a long breath before forcefully exhaling. 'That's how you operate. It must be in the family genes.'

Fonso stops chewing. His stare is unrelenting. This is the moment Zico fears most. He worries Fonso will finally lose patience with him.

Fonso offers, 'You had a fantastic day, right?'

Zico nods earnestly.

'Let's keep it that way. It means a lot to me, and a lot to you. Tonight, we have a truce. In the next couple of days, you will come clean. I want to know what's the truth from your perspective, what's irrefutable logic, and what's fanciful fiction?'

This encourages Zico to open up. 'I want to tell you the truth about my lies!'

Fonso's body stiffens.

Zico back-tracks at high speed. 'I haven't told a lie since I've been here. But I haven't been completely honest either.'

Fonso relaxes. He starts chewing on his bread again. 'I know. When you feel comfortable, you approach me. I promise you; I won't hit the roof. That will be a miracle, but I will try. This is my deal to you.'

Zico lets out a sigh. A tonne of weight is lifted from his shoulders.

They shake on the agreement. At first, Zico feels small and silly. Then his grandpa reaches up with his left hand and clasps Zico in a double-handshake. For the first time, he is equal to an adult. He looks up at the massive man in awe. Fonso has a purpose in everything he does, and this gesture is comforting and protective. *This surely is a moment to remember.*

What a day, he thinks, staring into the Deep Forest from his bunk. Rolling onto his back, Zico stares up at the cloudy sky. He contemplates how the random lightning bolts electrifying the horizon, mirror the drama of his day.

Zico jumps when his phone vibrates, announcing a message. *Zico. Never doubted your abilities.* A smiley face and thumbs up are added. Attached is a cheeky-faced selfie taken during the day at Sancia's penthouse.

It's a fun picture. Zico chuckles, then mutters under his breath, 'Girls.'

CHAPTER 9

PARADISE LOST

The predicted storm cell casts a spell over Roldão. Heavy rain and stronger than usual winds pound the coast all night long.

In the morning, Zico's first priority is to help clean up the courtyard and secure the new goal. Already outside, Fonso is piling up branches and leaves near the house.

Zico is concerned about the hidden equipment behind the boulder. He walks to the edge to check if it is exposed. To his relief, he cannot see it. His mood quickly changes to upbeat.

'I guess there goes football today,' Zico says.

Fonso assesses the sky. 'Not a chance, we never cancel anything here. This is just a little rain. Rain is water, and water is life.'

Already soaking wet from being outside for a moment, Zico runs, sneakers squelching, back to the house. He flops on his bunk and gazes at the dark grey clouds racing toward him. They are like bumper cars on a collision course. He is fascinated by Nothing Forever. It seems every aspect of this place is cloaked in drama.

Kneeling on all fours, Zico shakes himself like a shaggy dog after a bath. He spreads his damp around the room. Pressing his nose and mouth against the cold window, Zico expels his warm breath, creating his own clouds. He squiggles in them, before rubbing his doodles away and starting again.

No paper planes will fly today. There will be no fun with the jaguar. No new explorations. And, no buzz around an all but empty compound.

Fonso enters the house fully drenched, clothes sticking to his skin like cling wrap. With phone pressed to his ear, he paces, pivots on his heel, and re-traces his steps. Zico is amused by the water streaming down his legs, leaving small puddles in his wake.

As he catches his grandpa's vibe, he squirms on the bunk. When Fonso ceases talking, he stops walking. His grip on the phone tenses and his face screws into a frown.

Zico has not seen him this upset before. At least he is not causing the grief. All Zico picks up is a terse grumble, *'We'll see about that!'* before the connection is terminated. Stuffing the mobile in his trouser pocket, Fonso turns around, grabs a rain jacket, and walks out.

As quick as the door shuts, he returns a tad more composed. 'The game's on at five. See you then.'

'Everything alright?' Zico asks.

'Tell you tonight, once I know what's going on.' His voice is muffled by the closing door.

The silence is punctured by the unexpected tremble of Zico's mobile phone. It's Sancia. He jumps to his feet, tracking Fonso's path across the floorboards. The device vibrates in his hand. Zico wills himself to stay cool. He accepts the call. 'Who's this?' he blurts.

'Who else but me?' Sancia teases.

Zico pulls the mobile away from his ear, softly telling himself off as he stares at the screen. He attempts to regain his composure. 'Uh, hi Sancia, how are you?'

'All the rain is boring and uninspiring. What are you up to?'

'Nothing much. Although, there could be a problem with my tools to get in and out of the Deep Forest. Depending on where the storm blew them, people might work out what I've been up to. I don't need a spotlight on my adventures,' Zico confides.

After a short pause, Sancia asks, 'What do you need?'

'What I really need is a miracle!' Zico laughs, 'Can you magic up four emergency rope ladders, 10 metres long, some safety equipment with hooks, snowshoes, a backpack and some trekking poles?'

Rapid clicking thumps in his ears.

'Anything else?'

Zico stares at the phone. 'No! Are you for real? I was joking.'

'Uh, uh,' Sancia interjects. 'Go facetime, and look at the order.'

Obediently, Zico switches the call to facetime. Her 20-inch computer takes over his phone display. The purchase confirmation from a Brazilian adventure store lists all the items they talked about.

Sancia adds, 'Paid and express shipped.'

Dumbfounded, Zico flops on his back on the bunk. 'How can a twelve-year-old-girl spend eight thousand seven hundred forty-three Reais?' Zico gasps, eyes bulging at the screen. This is an insane amount. He never heard anyone talking about that much money. Or seen a person splash it out in a matter of seconds.

Sancia chimes in, 'Well, that's that, I guess. There's enough gear to take us down to the forest, right?'

Zico throws his hands to his head in utter disbelief of her intrusion on his adventure. The phone flies from his grip, bouncing from the window to the floor. He rolls on his belly, reaches down, and snaps it up in his shaking hand.

'Us, did you say, *us* ? To the Deep Forest. No. No way,' Zico argues. 'Won't be happening.'

Before he can talk sense into Sancia, she dismisses him. 'Why should I be stifled by my world? My parents are always telling me a good person knows their place, an interesting one seizes the opportunity. I do, on both counts! You're not the only one with a spirit of adventure. You're the guide I just hired.'

Zico blows hard, rolling his eyes.

Sancia ignores him. 'Tomorrow will be a fine day. So, courtesy of my mum's credit card, I've earned my place on your expedition team. The gear will arrive this afternoon. I'll stash it in the bushes overnight. Meet me at the hole in the wall at ten o'clock. From there, we make our way down to the forest. I can't wait for you to show me around!'

Zico groans.

'By the way, when I say ten, I mean ten.' She pauses for breath and almost whispers, 'Please, take me with you.'

'How can someone so pretty be so complicated?' Zico mumbles as he hangs up. He slides the phone under the pillow, then sits on it.

It takes an hour of pacing the house before Zico relents. Snatching up the phone, he opens her text with the cheeky selfie. He is smitten by her mischievousness. A silly smile spreads across his face as he looks at the photo. After a while, his focus shifts to the background. He enlarges the picture on the display screen.

Behind Sancia is the open door to the office, with a 3D model sitting on a table. He spotted the prototype yesterday. At the time, he took little notice of the design. Zico zooms in.

It replicates the volcano crater, but the Deep Forest is replaced by a luxurious 200-boat marina. There is also a clubhouse with elevators to transport Precious Above the Sea residents to and from their world. These lifts are set to the left of Fonso's courtyard, bypassing the prison tower. A massive tunnel is cut into the crater to connect the ocean to the dock.

Zico stares at the screen. Needing fresh air fast, he unhinges the bolt holding the bunk-robe's back panels together, and pushes the windows open. The rain is bucketing down. Zico holds his phone up to match the image to the forest's footprint. Desolated, he sinks into the bunk. Squeezing his eyes shut stems the flow of hot tears waiting to burst through.

★ ★ ★

Zico arrives at the colosseum, soaking wet. The weather transformed the hard soil on the pitch to mud. Joining his teammates, he is sluggish and glum in contrast to their excited chatter.

He tracks Fonso's entrance to the VIP lounge. *His mood is darker than the storm.* It occurs to him that Fonso always broods after speaking with his father. *This cannot be good. Was that Dad on the phone this morning about the school fire?*

Before he comes up with more theories, the game is on. The White Shirts are facing the Tribal Warriors. A physical and rough team with nothing to lose as they are placed bottom of the ladder. They are the losers of the losers', and they play like it.

The White Shirts triumph easily in the muddy arena. Yet, their performance was lacklustre, undermining the team's confidence to face their opponent in the upcoming relegation match. With only two shots in the vicinity of the net, Zico's goalie skills were not tested.

After the longest and hottest shower ever, Zico strolls back into the house. Fonso waits for him at the table, dinner prepared and plated. To engage Fonso in the conversation, Zico makes his dull day sound like the best he ever had.

Finally, Zico finds the courage to ask, 'Something wrong, Fonso? Anything to do with me?'

Realising how his mood affects Zico, Fonso is gentle with the boy. 'This is business. Just a force I need to sort out, which I thought would never cross the line. It's complex.' Fonso's thin smile is not reassuring. 'On a positive note, tomorrow is a fine day and you can roam around again.'

Zico does not think that is a good thing. Sancia's family is involved in developing the Deep Forest into a marina. It will destroy the jaguar's habitat and intrude on Nothing Forever. He is unsure how to cope with that and Sancia. He reverts to his standard default position, ignoring his feelings. He'll deal with them at some other time.

★ ★ ★

Ten o'clock sharp, Zico pushes his head through the wall, bumping into the hidden equipment. Sancia is waiting next to it.

Zico whispers, 'We're not going.'

Frustrated, Sancia struggles to keep her voice down. 'Yes, we are!' she hisses. 'Why else would you come here?'

Zico pulls himself up into the bush. 'To talk to you in person and put some sense in your head.'

'We're going,' Sancia insists.

'Why is this so important?'

'Because I'm not allowed to go anywhere! Not to Nothing Forever, not to the Deep Forest. It is way too restrictive. Plus, you've been down there. If you can do it, so can I! Let's see if the jaguar is for real.'

'You're talking about a wild animal; he could tear you apart. I got lucky so far.' Zico tries to scare her off.

'He won't, because he doesn't exist.' Sancia stands, swinging a backpack over her shoulder. 'Zico, this is not a debating comp, let's go.'

She pushes him back through the wall, practically shoving the gear at him.

Sancia chatters away. 'Jaguars are the keeper of the unknown. They are secretive, loyal, strong, beautiful, and they possess spiritual power, unlike any other animal. They live in silence and rejuvenate as they apply courage.'

Zico interrupts, 'How do you know all this?'

She stops in her tracks and turns around. 'I love reading about all kinds of things. So, I have the knowledge and the resources, and you have the skills and heart to get us in and out of there. Right?'

Zico is impressed with her determination, but remains unconvinced.

They stand at the edge, right above the prison guard tower rooftop. The new equipment is piled up next to them in the confined space. The tins of paint and the rope survived the storm. *At least that's one thing going in my favour.*

Zico grabs her shoulder to make sure he has her attention. 'We've got to be quiet. The guards have increased their patrols.'

She giggles. 'This is so exciting!'

'Listen, Sancia. This is not a game.' Zico emphasises, 'We are about to climb down a prison wall in a no-go zone.'

'Okay! I get it.'

Scanning Sancia from head to toe, he widens his eyes at her outfit: white platform sneakers, pink sequinned top, and designer three-quarter length body-hugging shorts. He thinks, *those clothes are more appropriate for a birthday party, than covertly exploring the Deep Forest.*

'What?' Sancia stares back at him.

For fifteen minutes, he explains how deadly the quicksand is and how vicious the jaguar can be. Nothing he says will deter her from taking the plunge.

Surrendering, he leads Sancia down the cliff face. Much longer than needed, the unravelled ladder is sucked into position. Zico carries the backpack with the second ladder protruding. Snowshoes and trekking poles are strapped to them. Hanging by one hand, Zico clips the two ladders together. He rolls out the apparatus, by-passing the unforgiving quicksand. They navigate it with ease, then use the snowshoes to glide-walk across the sand.

Once they store their climbing aids in a safe place, Zico checks the surroundings. Sancia is unimpressed. She thinks Zico is making fun of her being afraid of a jaguar that does not exist. She spots the thread paving the way into the forest.

'Here's the string,' Sancia calls out. 'You have been down here.'

'That's what I've been telling you,' Zico replies.

As Zico and Sancia follow the string through the bushes, branches snap nearby. Catching up to Zico, Sancia grabs his hand. He doesn't like it but cannot shake her off.

He laughs, 'Here comes the jaguar.'

Within a flash, the big cat leaps at him. He falls backward with a thud and rolls around on the ground. Sancia studies Zico, wondering what he is doing. Zico pats the jaguar who is reluctant at first, tilting his head toward Sancia.

'This is Sancia. She's kind of a friend of mine,' he explains. He is teasing Sancia. She thinks he is being weird.

'Kind of,' she mimics. 'Who are you talking to?'

Zico turns to her with one arm still around his pal. 'The jaguar,' he frowns.

'There is no jaguar. I can't see a jaguar. One giant adventure into the Deep Forest, one giant imagination for boykind,' Sancia laughs. 'You had me for a moment. You were so full-on at the top of the cliff. I started to think I should worry about your ferocious imaginary friend.'

Zico studies Sancia's expression, trying to work her out. Rubbing his eyes, Zico returns his gaze to the jaguar. He is clearly visible. Taking her hand, he places it on the jaguar's head. Together they stroke it. Zico loves the feel of its rough fur. Sancia rolls her eyes and grimaces.

'Okay Zico, the joke's over.'

Stunned, Zico steps back as the jaguar sits, tilts his head, and steadies his eyes at her. *What's real, what's not?* Zico is becoming more and more confused.

'He is here, right here,' he stammers.

As Sancia walks off, she calls over her shoulder. 'That is not funny, Zico. I don't like being ridiculed.'

Zico runs after her. He grudgingly accepts she cannot see the jaguar. 'You never believed he existed, right?' he yells.

'Right, because you are making this stuff up.'

Zico catches up. His furry friend trailing them like an obedient pet. 'I was truthful about the Deep Forest. The jaguar is for real too!'

Sancia's eyes somersault.

'Hear me out,' he pleads. 'I want you to believe it, I really want you to try.'

Sancia releases a heavy sigh and stares at him.

'Please, there's something magical about this place. It's sort of spiritual. Just go with it.'

Sancia gives in. They stroll off, with the jaguar following close behind.

They reach the Tree of Love and Zico encourages her to hug it. For the first time, Sancia relaxes and is within the moment. They enter the Bay of Plenty, mesmerising Sancia instantly. She is immersed in its tranquility, natural beauty, and vibrant colours. In sheer happiness, she throws her arms around Zico, squeezing him in a cuddle. *Awkward!* When Sancia turns around, she faces the jaguar and yelps.

Zico realises immediately that she surrendered to the power of the forest. Raising her hand hesitantly, she gently strokes wild cat. When he responds kindly, Zico joins in. The jaguar purrs contentedly.

'What's his name?' Sancia asks.

'Jaguar.'

'That's not a name. Jaguar is a species. Remarkable, you name everything else around here but not the most precious resident of this beautiful place.'

Zico gives an embarrassed shrug. Sancia scans the environment, taking everything in. Finally, she declares, 'He should be called Boondi.'

Zico turns to her, then to the jaguar. 'Boondi?'

'Yes, Boondi,' she nods confidently. The jaguar paces proudly towards them, slightly tilting his head.

'Where does Boondi come from?' Zico questions.

'If you were present when at school, then maybe you would know,' Sancia teases. 'Australia's Indigenous people around Sydney speak of it. It means water breaking over rocks. Look around, that's what this place is all about. His habitat. This rock pool is sculptured from the flow of water.'

Zico mutters, 'And you learned all that in school?'

He repeats the name a few times, liking the sound of it. 'A perfect fit. Let's play with Boondi.'

For the next hour, they swim and enjoy their time together.

Sometime later they are at the spot where the dense forest meets the sand dune. Sancia and Zico are ready to depart. They wear snowshoes to trek up the crater. Before setting off, they cuddle Boondi goodbye. Next to the quicksand they remove the snowshoes and strap them with the trekking poles to their backpacks. They climb carefully over the sand-trap to reach the vertical ladder which takes them up the cliff's face.

Exhausted and relieved, both stand on the cliff ledge, out of sight from the courtyard. They take a moment to appreciate their adventure. Zico rolls up the ladders neatly and stores their equipment in the gap.

Sancia gives Zico a crushing hug. 'Thanks for making this day one of my best ever. The forest is unspoiled by everything else around here. It will be our secret place, Zico.'

He turns his head away, wringing his hands with worry.

'Why are you upset?'

Zico pulls the phone from the backpack. He points out the background of her photo and the model of a marina. Sancia is shocked. Her eyes travel from the image to the sweeping view of the forest below and back again.

She protests, 'I've seen that a million times and never realised what it means.'

CHAPTER 10

FACTS, TRUTHS AND FICTION

As the sun sets, Fonso and Zico eat dinner in the courtyard. Lost in thought, Zico picks at the food on his plate. He half listens to Fonso prattle on about the relegation match in a few days' time; the winners' comp is still being played out. His curiosity is sparked when Fonso diverts to the past, present, and future of Nothing Forever. Zico rewards him with his full attention.

In the last couple of days, Fonso has been confronted with choices that will affect the community. Many years ago, they went through a pacification process. The idea was to be more integrated with society and to remove the dangerous gangs running the neighbourhood. Fonso followed a moderate path and emerged as their leader.

He concedes an element of crime still exists, which he tolerates. The stolen BMW and its disposal are an example. To improve schooling and services, as well as economic prospects, much more is required. A common cause is needed to unite the people to move forward.

'It's like nation building on a small scale,' Fonso says.

'Why are you so worried?'

'Without any notice, the local government withdrew our funding, and we can't work out why. Something big is brewing and it is putting the village at risk. Without the money, I will lose control and the bad old ways will creep back in. When that happens, the forces will be deployed to bulldoze the place. It's prime real estate.'

Zico's eyes widen as he connects the dots. The marina project will wipe out the hillside village. The government will tear down homes, causing a backlash. This will be viewed as a riot, giving them a reason to get rid of everyone. They will cover up the development, and no one will care.

The rich, privilege, and power will win over the poor, excluded, and helpless. *Now is the right time to open up to Fonso.* Zico takes a deep breath and loudly blows away any doubts.

He clears his throat. 'Ah hmm. Fonso. Remember we talked about values, principles, and interests, and how they affect things.'

'Of course, it's a constant battle,' Fonso says.

Zico continues, 'And you said whatever I tell you, you won't be hopping mad.'

Fonso straightens up, presses his lips together, and then corrects his grandson. 'I said, I'll try not to hit the roof.'

'That's good intention, right?' Zico asks.

'Alright, what is going on?' Fonso struggles to maintain his patience but falls short. 'Is this about the school fire?'

Zico says, 'You know how things are sometimes mixed up between truth, fact, and fiction. How some people pick anything that works to explain their actions, so they feel better.'

The weight of Zico's words hits Fonso. He leans forward and very slowly says, 'Yes.'

'Well, I never lied...' Zico says.

Fonso cuts him short, finishing his sentence. 'But you never told the whole truth either.'

Zico nods.

Fonso presses, 'So?'

'So, here we go...'

Zico explains himself, telling the full story for the first time. His half-truths started when a kid kicked his football into the Deep Forest. Zico did not want to let him down by losing the gift. Especially because Fonso made such a huge effort to source it. So, he went down to the forest, several times, and returned alive.

The mystery of why no one ever came back from the Deep Forest is solved. He found skeletons in the quicksand at the top of the crater. His actions did not cause the volcano to blow up. He describes how he beat the deadly sandpit. And, he explains how the Deep Forest is an amazing ecosystem, needing protection.

Unable to fully break from his old ways, Zico holds back details. He leaves Sancia and Boondi out of his storytelling.

With a massive sigh, Zico slumps back and nervously waits for Fonso's response. His tense face pre-warns Zico of an outburst. Somehow, Fonso calms his emotions.

'It's all my fault, Zico,' Fonso finally declares.

'Your fault?'

'I set an expectation about the ball. It was way off. Would you have gone down there if I hadn't?'

'No, I don't think so,' Zico answers.

'You can't tell anyone about this. The people will believe you are cursed. Superstition beats logic. This could mean the end for you and me here. Do you understand, Zico?'

Shocked to silence, all Zico can do is nod.

Shaking his head Fonso murmurs, 'You're lucky you didn't die! I would never forgive myself.' He eyeballs Zico. 'Does anyone else know about these trips?'

Zico tells him about the kid who kicked the ball.

Fonso weighs up all he has been told. 'His word against yours. You are a reliable, selective truth-teller,' he reasons. 'Plus, you're the Patrão's grandson.'

'And, Sancia,' Zico mumbles.

'Sancia? Who's she?'

'A girl I became friends with.'

'How does she fit into this? I've never met anyone by that name and I know everyone!' The worry in Fonso's voice fills the room.

Zico explains how they got tangled up. She lives at Precious Above the Sea, and together they explored the Deep Forest.

Now, Fonso hits the roof.

He stands, towering over Zico, with fists clenched at his sides. His whole body trembles. 'You and me, we may get away with you going into the forest. We can control it.' Shaking his finger at the fence high above their heads, Fonso leans over him. 'But going up there is unforgivable! I will call your father to pick you up. You are out of here. I'm done.'

Fonso storms into the house and slams the door, leaving Zico stunned.

A message from Sancia appears on the mobile: *I had no idea Zico. Never took any interest in what Dad builds. I'll do anything to stop this. Please call me when you can.*

Snivelling at his treachery and Fonso's extreme reaction, Zico enters the house. He struggles to carry all the dishes at once. Fonso is at the table, about to contact his son. Zico drops the plates with a loud clunk into the kitchen sink.

He sniffles, 'Don't Fonso. Please. Let me stay here to help solve your problem.'

Fonso snorts his disgust. 'Solve my problem? You, Zico, are my problem.'

Pulling out his phone, Zico shows Fonso Sancia's photo.

Fonso checks the picture. He comments, 'Cute. So, you're in love?'

Dismayed, Zico pleads, 'No, no. Look at what's behind her in the office.'

Fonso expands the image and studies the 3D model as Zico argues his case.

'The reason the government pulled your funds is for you to go back to the old dysfunctional ways. Kind of clever. The Precious Above the Sea people want to extend their territory to Precious by the Sea. A new flashy marina that will wipe out the village.'

Fonso turns to Zico, pulling him into a bear hug; suffocating and welcoming at the same time. Closing his eyes, Zico throws his arms around his grandpa. He wholeheartedly returns the embrace.

'Well done, Zico. Now I know what and who we're up against. I guess you'll be staying here a bit longer,' he says.

Zico shows him a photo he took at the Bay of Plenty. Fonso is awestruck. 'No one has ever seen this place, but you and Sancia.'

'How's that possible?' Zico asks.

Fonso explains, 'The curse and myths. And, the prison next door, which means no drones are allowed in the airspace. Take your pick.'

'How can someone build something without detailed plans of the area?' Zico asks.

'Our life is not measured by money, but others decide our worth by our lack of it.' Fonso scoffs, 'Money is the only interest of developers.'

Zico's turbulent day comes to an end. Just before he falls asleep in the bunk, he replies to Sancia's message: *Let's talk in the morning.*

★ ★ ★

The next day, Zico gets up to the sound of men talking in the courtyard. He recognises Fonso's commanding voice.

Fonso is with a very round man who Zico guesses is at least in his fifties. They gather around the table smothered by maps, council guidelines, and legal papers.

Zico joins the meeting, greeting the men with a tired, 'Morning.'

'You must be Zico!' the man guesses.

'That's me.' Zico's eyes wander over the comical-looking visitor. Suspenders at full strain over a balloon belly. Jolly-looking face lit up by inquisitive eyes. Hair ringing his head like a crown. Zico surmises *this is an influential man.*

'Everyone calls me De Sousa. I can bend the law, depending on the price or the cause. In this case, it's the cause. Now, Fonso told me all about your misadventures, so no need to pretend.'

Head whipping from De Sousa to Fonso and back again, Zico is slightly on edge.

'Listen, if you are ever in trouble, I'll get you off the hook.' De Sousa swiftly pulls his business card from his shirt pocket and hands it over.

Zico takes a seat, pouring himself a glass of orange juice, and listens to their discussion. For the village to block the development, they must gain a vote in the council. Even with a show of hands, a motion to stop the marina will be awfully close. Most likely, they face defeat.

Going by what De Sousa says, Zico works out he is the best lawyer around. The issue is, Precious Above the Sea has the power and money to buy council approvals. Up until now, they kept the marina project quiet.

'Why can't you vote?' Zico interjects.

'Because this place is illegal, not officially recognised. I'll give you one-hundred Reais if you can find it on the map.'

De Sousa sweeps his hand across the official chart of the region. No buildings exist where the village is located.

'The fact is, Nothing Forever needs to become something significant fast. To survive, it must be a government certified community. We need to register an official population count, elect a mayor, and name the walkways. This means being on the grid with electricity, water, and a sewer system. This place deserves a respectful name that is used by all. We need everything executed within a couple of days, or this place is history.'

With mouth stretched, De Sousa pants from his assessment of the effort ahead. His jolly face morphs into a grisly scene.

Zico asks, 'We can do this, right?'

'Do you want me to make some phone calls?' De Sousa looks grimly at Fonso, who gives his nod of approval.

CHAPTER 11

THE HARD WAY

Although De Sousa left long ago, his gloomy outlook is imprinted on Fonso's face. Pushing himself up from the table, he swipes at the papers. Moving to the edge of the courtyard, Fonso stares thoughtfully into the forest. He wonders if this is the end of it all. *How can a spiritual place present such a bleak future?*

Lying on his bunk with windows open, Zico gazes into the Deep Forest, seeking wisdom. Phone squashed between his shoulder and ear, he talks with Sancia about stopping the development. Zico cautions her that saving the forest could mean losing her dad's trust. She confirms her commitment to the cause. The forest must be saved. Sancia promises she will ask her dad a few questions about the marina.

Ending the call, Zico monitors the phone's battery power, which is down to 51%. With a quick roll, he pushes himself off the bunk. Springing over to Fonso's computer, he checks the cable extension. Sancia's phone is an older version, and the charger is incompatible. *Doesn't matter. There's plenty of juice left in it.*

A short time later, Zico joins Fonso outside. He reviews Fonso's strategic plan which needs to be actioned within three days. If all goes well, this will enable them to cast a vote against the marina.

72 HOURS
Go public — oppose marina — become a town
Population count — official
Mayor elected — me
Name walkways and mark buildings
Electricity — meters established — bills to be provided
Running water — meters installed and corroborated
Sewer working — pass demonstration
New name for the community?

Fonso assures Zico, 'We'll give it a shot. The last thing they expect from us is to live within the law. Doing things by the book gives us the authority to vote the marina down. Now, here comes the million Reais question: can we trust Sancia?'

Zico is convinced she will not let them down as she found a connection with the Deep Forest. Fonso accepts his judgement. However, the moment he registers the community with the council, the developers will be alerted. Let the battle begin.

Armed with his phone, Fonso mobilises the local TV station and the entire village. Between calls, he outlines his plan to Zico.

'Attack is the best defence. I'll yank my town managers off their lazy backsides and allocate the projects.'

Zico is heartened by his decisiveness.

Striding toward the gate, Fonso is a man on a mission. He yells over his shoulder, 'Uh, by the way, all football is cancelled until this is sorted. Which means the teams stay where they are.'

Zico throws his head back and groans. He understands it is a necessary loss for any chance of a greater victory.

Unnoticed, Sancia sneaks across the courtyard. On her tippy-toes, she approaches Zico from behind, without a sound, and covers his eyes with her hands. Taken by surprise, he lashes out. Swinging his arms and legs wildly, he is like a bull in a rodeo. Sancia is on his back, squealing with joy.

Realising it is her, he stops bucking. Zico is not pleased to see her. He challenges, 'What are you doing here?'

'I'm here to help. There's no one up there,' she pouts. 'I thought it'd be more fun here with you, Zico.' Swivelling her head to take in the sights, she smiles sweetly at him. 'So, has Fonso calmed down?'

They hear Fonso before they see him. 'Zico, have you seen my phone?'

As Fonso strides toward them, Sancia dives under the table, taking cover.

'Fonso, or for you, Patrão, has settled alright,' he confirms. 'Come-on out. You shouldn't be here.'

Sancia crawls out from her hiding spot, looking up at Fonso. 'Nor should you, but here we are.'

Zico almost faints, knowing Fonso's very small fuse is likely to ignite an explosive temper.

Head whipping, Fonso takes a second look at the girl, 'Come again.'

Squinting through the glare of the sun, she holds Fonso's gaze. 'I said, nor should you, but here we are.'

'You trust her?' Fonso questions Zico.

Eyes bulging and mouth agape, Zico nods.

Fonso turns back to Sancia. 'You must be Sancia?'

She offers her hand in greeting. 'Sancia Della Rossa.'

'You stole my line. I always say, no one wants us to be here, but here we are.' Fonso snorts. 'Now, let me tell you something else. Some of us are not even accounted for. They don't even hold a bank account. Did you know one in three Brazilians don't have banking credentials? That's 45 million people which amounts to 800 billion Reais a year in cash only activities. We're real, we're somebody, and we're not shadows. So, why are you here?'

'I want to help you to make sure Dad doesn't build the marina and destroy the Deep Forest.'

Zico's head swivels from Sancia to Fonso, awaiting a verdict.

Fonso cautions, 'You know what the consequences are when your father finds out you were here? What do you think he'll do when he works out you helped us to defeat his project?'

Sancia's head drops slightly. She doesn't like what he is saying, and is not sure she wants to hear him out.

Fonso continues. 'It could cost you your relationship with him, not to mention tonnes of money. It's a high price to pay.'

After a long silence, Sancia meekly utters, 'Our bond is not that strong. We're usually not on the same wavelength. My Dad complains I don't do anything worthwhile. He thinks I'm all opinion and no substance.' She pauses. 'I think, the benefit outweighs the risk.'

Fonso turns to Zico, then back to her. 'Zico trusts you, you know?' With a hint of nostalgia, he remarks, 'Twenty years ago I would have held you hostage for ransom. Forcing your parents to give me 1 million Reais to drop the development. Lucky for you, I've changed a bit. I now do things the hard way. The next three days will be a testament to that.'

Fonso grabs his phone and shouts back at Zico as he walks off to the gate. 'She's your problem, Zico. Outfit her in something more suitable for the occasion. On the table is a map of the village. Make up some names for the walkways and passages, and number every container and shed.'

Sancia is inspected from top to toe by Zico. He shakes his head in agreement with Fonso. She wears a designer dress, expensive looking sneakers, and has fresh flowers pinned in her hair. Realising her inappropriate choice of clothes, Sancia is self-conscious. Zico's body shudders with suppressed laughter.

'Don't look at me that way,' she tells him off.

Zico gently slaps her shoulder, 'Fonso's right. You'll never go unnoticed dressed like that.' Zico nods his head in the direction of the house. She silently follows him.

When Sancia reappears, she is transformed from cocktail-cool to slum-chic. This accomplishment is achieved by a pair of Zico's cargo shorts, hanging baggy from her hips. Even with an old T-shirt, no shoes, and a baseball cap, his gear appears upmarket on her. To complete the styling, Zico smudges some dirt on her perfectly clean skin.

They spread the map on the table, securing each corner with a cup. Standing on the chair to lean over it, Zico runs his finger across the chart. He points out the endless walkways and passages, the colosseum, and the cogwheel track. From this angle, the squiggles are like a giant ball of spaghetti. The houses on the blueprint are marked by hand-drawn squares. They give no indication of how many sheds there are.

'This plan makes no sense,' Sancia objects.

'Let's do what we can for now. We'll start by naming the walkways. That can't be too hard. I'll chart them and you list them on a separate piece of paper,' Zico encourages her.

'Who put you in charge?' Sancia challenges.

'Whatever,' Zico shoots back.

'Okay,' she back-tracks, 'as long as I can name every second walkway. Deal?'

'I tell you if you weren't so pretty,' Zico catches himself. 'Uh, I mean...'

'You think I'm attractive — the old or the new version?' She gets up and twirls around giggling.

Zico takes a deep breath to regain his cool. 'We'll take turns, one at a time. You start.' He mumbles under his breath, 'That'll shut you up!'

For the next two hours, they come up with sixty-three quirky names for the alleys of the hillside village. Twelve deserve mention:

Patrão's Place
Flippy Lane
Colosseum Junction
Yellow Passage
Butterfly Way
Dead-End Alley
Mystic Maze
Ghost Crescent
Sorcerer Lane

Emerald Steps
Twinkle Terrace
Lost Avenue

Both are very pleased with their creations. They take off to wander around the village and allocate the numbers, shed by shed. Sancia has never seen anything as poor as this.

Posters to vote for mayor, featuring a mug shot of a much younger Fonso, are plastered all around. At times, she openly stares at people, needing Zico to nudge her back to work. When boys take notice of her, he becomes protective, seemingly growing a few inches and staring them down.

Zico takes photos of Sancia in the walkways, standing right in front of one of the posters. The phone's battery is down to 36%.

The colosseum is turned into a temporary registration area. Tables and chairs are scattered around for the official counting to take place. The other half of the stadium is converted for joinery production to build street signs, house numbers, and letterboxes. Sancia is fascinated by the spirit of these people and how efficiently they are deployed.

Nearby, several TV reporters record a statement drafted by De Sousa and read out by Fonso. Sancia and Zico tune in and learn from Fonso's tactics. By announcing how they were duped about the proposed marina, they'll win over public opinion. This will force the Roldão Council to be compliant and operate within the law, or so they think.

Zico and Sancia return to the courtyard. They finalise their designs on huge sheets of paper. Inspired by the Deep Forest, they create symbols like a jaguar's paw, birds and flowers, to decorate the signage.

Fonso arrives, highly motivated with an army of helpers. He casts his eyes over the map and is impressed with the output. 'Well done.'

Handing the artwork to one of his underlings he instructs, 'Have these printed within a day. Production must start immediately. Work through the night until the job is complete. Without these signs on the walls, we're not legal.'

The helper rolls up the papers, stuffing them under his arm. He pushes through the crowd, heading for the stairway.

Taking a moment, Fonso appreciates the purpose and teamwork of the people. He scans the sea of faces, acknowledging their contribution with a warm smile. He is caught by surprise when his eyes fall on Sancia, who he almost doesn't recognise.

'What a transformation, almost one of us!'

'What's missing?' Sancia's head drops, devastated at the thought of not fitting in.

'The pain of never knowing where your next Real comes from,' Fonso replies.

Zico rolls his eyes and broadcasts his disapproval with a shake of his head.

Raising his hands in surrender, Fonso apologises, 'Sorry Sancia.'

'Why are you making the signs here? Wouldn't it be faster to have them done by a proper sign maker?' Zico asks.

Fonso says, 'Every possible sabotage must be considered and eliminated. The more we control our own destiny, the less likely we will fail.'

Surrounded by his team, including Zico and Sancia, Fonso runs through his list. He acknowledges De Sousa's arrival with a wave. Hooking his finger repeatedly, he indicates De Sousa should join him at the front.

'Two days left to go public and oppose the marina.' Fonso's voice is gravelly and full of emotion. Clearing his throat, he declares, 'We will rise from the rubble to emerge as a town. Our residents will vote.'

De Sousa queries, 'You are the only candidate?'

Fonso confirms, 'I will become Mayor!'

Everyone claps in agreement.

'So, where is the planning at?' De Sousa asks.

Fonso uses his fingers to count off the tasks still to be done. 'We have named the walkways, we now need to mark the buildings. Electricity and water meters are being installed. We'll work out later how to pay for them! The sewer network is our advantage, but we must pass a test. Uh, and we need a new name for the town.'

De Sousa's silence is concerning.

Bewildered, Fonso asks, 'What now?'

'The sewer test is our Achilles heel,' he warns.

Fonso silences him with a swipe of his hand. 'We have a sewer system that works, the first in Bahia! If I'm remembered for anything — and it should be carved into my gravestone — it's this sewer system.'

Fonso visualises his granite tombstone shaped like a toilet wall mount with a flusher attached to it. Several sewer pipes extend from his grave. He quickly snaps back to reality, not amused by the vision.

'The sewer system is the only thing in place and you tell me it's not compliant?' Fonso barks, 'What are you talking about?'

De Sousa explains, 'The council made a new ruling for developments. Every new town must have a pressure circuit installed.' He squirms, 'To push poo down from the highest outlet to the main sewer grid. And, within one minute, or it won't be approved.'

Fonso takes a seat, his whole-body deflating. 'See what money can buy you!' He glares at Sancia. She shrinks at his comments. Zico steps in, shielding her.

Fonso knows he overstepped the mark. 'Sorry Sancia.'

The silence is suffocating. Everyone but De Sousa stares awkwardly at their feet. De Sousa shuffles under the weight of his round body. He moves from the table to the bathroom and back, waving his arms around as he theorises, 'This is the highest toilet.' He walks to the ledge and leans around to his right to see the distance. 'It needs to go down there, right?'

De Sousa turns around, facing the group, and shakes his head in defeat.

Fonso throws his hands in the air. 'Even if we slingshot the poo down there, it'd take more than a minute.'

A whiney chorus of 'Ewww' echoes. Noses wrinkle and brows scrunch in disgust.

'They really want us to fail,' Sancia concedes.

Zico has an idea. 'No way. How about if we build a pipe going straight down there, using the footprint of the cogwheel structure. It's the most direct route. Connect a pressure pump and blast it down. All we need then is to join the pipe to the sewer line at the bottom. That's the spot to prove timing.'

Sancia interrupts. 'The issue is, how do we get a pipe directly from here to the top of the cogwheel?'

Zico counters, 'Well, it's obvious, isn't it?' He rubs his hands together and grins madly at his audience. 'We'll need to go through some houses.'

A long silence follows.

It sounds so crazy it makes perfect sense. Fonso dances a jig and everyone laughs as they celebrate such a simple yet brilliant concept.

Grabbing pen and paper, Zico draws the buildings at the top of the village. The first line links Fonso's toilet to the cogwheel, through several houses on a modest slope. At the upper cable car platform, below a grill, Zico draws an arrow and writes *pump*. A long diagonal line follows the cogwheel track from top to bottom. A slight bend connects this line to the main sewer pipe.

'Will that beat the requirements?' Fonso asks De Sousa.

He gives a prompt nod, 'As long as it beats 60 seconds.' De Sousa chuckles, slapping his knee, 'Ahh, I can feel the anticipation building for the inaugural Bahia bog-sledding race.'

Fonso dials a number as he shouts, 'This will be an all-nighter.'

Everyone scurries like an intrusion of cockroaches escaping pesticides.

Fonso takes Sancia and Zico aside. He apologises to her and thanks them for helping. Sancia's phone rings. She stares at it for a moment before disconnecting the call. 'I need to go home,' she pouts. Spinning on her heels, she hurries across the courtyard toward the cliff wall.

Zico follows her. About to say goodbye, a smirk forms on his face.

'What?' Sancia demands.

Zico eyes her up and down, suppressing the laughter that threatens to erupt. 'Hey, you make my stuff cool, but I think this could freak your family out.'

Sancia looks down at herself, realising she is still in disguise. 'Oh,' she grins back. 'I suspect you're right. I do look like a grubby little caterpillar, don't I?' Sancia sprints to the house, emerging as a beautiful butterfly, and flutters up the cliff face.

CHAPTER 12

CONQUER AND UNITE

F onso answers a call, looking briefly at Zico before moving to the far side of the courtyard. Listening more than talking, he offers the occasional grunt — message understood. Zico glances sideways, trying to eavesdrop. He finds it hard to tell if Fonso is pleased or upset. Moments later, Fonso wraps up the conversation, 'I'll see you then.' He peers out at the forest, deep in thought.

Turning to Zico, Fonso waves him over to share the news. Zico's parents will pick him up the day after tomorrow. Grinning from ear to ear, Zico whoops, 'Alright!' Only now is he willing to admit how much he misses his family.

Fonso studies the boy with a kindly smile, then pulls him in for a hug. As Zico returns the squeeze, his broad grin fades into a tremble. Zico buries his head in Fonso's chest.

He sniffles, 'That means I have to leave the village, the Deep Forest, and you.'

Fonso comforts him. 'You'll always have the bunk in my house, Zico.'

'So, we meet them on the outskirts again?' Zico lets out a sigh.

Fonso shakes his head. 'No, they're coming here.'

'Here, really?'

'Well, apparently they've seen enough good stuff about the village on TV and think we're a better community now. Go figure!' Fonso says.

Sitting on his bunk, Zico sends a message to Sancia. He lets her know how much he enjoyed hanging out with her today. Mindful that the battery power is low, now at 15%, he switches the phone off for the night.

From the kitchen Fonso calls out, 'Zico, I forgot to tell you. They arrested some local guy for burning down the school.'

Zico replies smugly, 'Told you so.'

All night long, Zico tosses and turns in his sleep. Fonso's people work at a hectic pace to complete the water and electricity meters. The making of signage and letterboxes reaches 50% of the final output. New pipes are installed within the steep cable car structure.

* * *

The next morning, several teenagers dig into the sewer line at the bottom of the village. Zico assists to fit a pump below the top-end of the cogwheel platform. To the dismay of some residents, a path is cut through kitchens, living rooms, bathrooms, and bedrooms.

Sancia works with Zico, telling helpers where to place street signs. They take selfies with the quirky signage in the background. Zico's phone indicates a 6% battery life.

In the colosseum, the hillside population is counted by the Office of Statista. At the same time, the people vote for Fonso to be mayor. A group of suited bureaucrats roam the maze of lanes. They sneer in disgust as they inspect and record the street signs and house numbers. The utility meters are tested and deemed compliant.

In the courtyard, Fonso strategises with De Sousa. Playing devil's advocate, they think about the tactics the developers will use to sabotage the sewer pipe test. The compliance check must fail for the marina to proceed.

De Sousa cautions, 'We need to assume the council will support the project. It means wealth and power to them.'

'What can they do to us that we can't prevent?' Fonso asks.

De Sousa retrieves three small stainless-steel containers from his briefcase, each a different colour: red, blue, and green. 'They'll use a container like one of these, but we won't know the colour.'

'Does the colour matter?'

'Absolutely.' De Sousa responds.

'Why?'

'The Flushing Committee announced a foolproof system, so we can't rig the outcome of the test. Only the head flusher is privy to which colour will be used,' De Sousa stresses.

Fonso cringes, 'Are you for real?'

'They're scared it will be flushed to the bottom in under 60 seconds.' De Sousa thinks for a moment. 'If I were them, I'd do one of two things: make the container disintegrate, or detonate it. Either option will happen just after it enters the sewer system. Game over.'

'Anything else I need to know?' Fonso snaps.

Unruffled, De Sousa states, 'Yep. Just to make it a bit more complicated, they insist no phones are allowed in your bathroom. When they flush, they'll fire a starter gun from the window and the clock will start ticking.'

Fonso grumbles, 'There must be someone else who knows the colour of the tin.'

'Well, the word is that the project owner wriggled himself into the decision-making process, like the worm he is. I hear he's so worried, he demanded to be the head flusher,' snorts De Sousa.

Fonso picks up the container, waving it about. 'Once we know the colour, it doesn't matter what they do. We'll pump down a replica from the top of the cogwheel.'

'Very clever,' De Sousa says.

Fonso concedes, 'This is all a pipe dream unless we know what colour it is.'

De Sousa purses his lips. 'The question is, is Zico's playmate on our side?'

On cue, Zico and Sancia arrive at the table in high spirits. Fonso and De Sousa stare at each other. They turn to Sancia, who raises an eyebrow.

'Were you talking about me?' she asks.

Both men nod. Fonso explains their predicament. Sancia insists on going back home to convince her father she should select the colour. After all, he is always harping on about her being more interested in his work. Then, all she needs to do is text the chosen colour to Zico.

★ ★ ★

Several hours later, a staged Candomblé themed celebration is underway. It creates noise and deflection. The visiting councillors swell with pride. They believe the festivities are in their honour.

Zico hides beneath the cogwheel platform. The cable car continues to travel up and down, adding to the commotion. An extra pump is in place and ready to be activated. Zico's job is to put the right container in the gap in the pipe. He stares at his dead phone, willing battery life into it. It's no use. *What's the colour, Sancia?*

Fonso stands with council members next to the foul-smelling sewer junction at the bottom of the village. One official puts a fishing net into the hole. Another bureaucrat readies the stopwatch. They are brimming with confidence.

A chauffeur-driven black Mercedes limousine arrives, stopping next to the official party. Sancia's father, Eduardo Della Rossa, steps out. He is a tall, elegantly dressed man. For this occasion, he is without a jacket. He carries a solid briefcase handcuffed to his wrist. Della Rossa offers a smug smile when he shakes Fonso's hand. Bulbs flash as the media witness the introductions.

'May the best plan win,' Della Rossa declares.

They shake hands once more while the press takes photos.

Sancia's father travels up the cliff in the cogwheel car. The cabin stops at the top, right above Zico, who spies on him from below the grill.

When Sancia's father enters Fonso's toilet chamber, he is taken by surprise. *How can such an exquisitely designed bathroom be in this derelict place?*

He unlocks and opens the briefcase which holds three coloured containers. A government official rests the starter gun on the ledge of the bathroom window. Della Rossa picks up the red container, drops it into the toilet, and flushes it.

The gunshot rings through the village. Everyone starts clapping and counting the seconds, '1, 2, 3, 4...'

In his hiding spot beneath the cable car platform, Zico realises he stuffed up. *It doesn't matter how great the plan is, if you can't get the small details right.* He yells, 'Stupid, stupid, stupid!'

Zico is stuck in a void where time stands still.

Seconds later, the pipe shudders. Water spews out of the toilet bowl. Della Rossa comments with a sly smile, 'Must be a blockage!'

De Sousa nods politely. 'It always sounds like that. It's not a perfect world.'

The water gushes out.

'But it does clean your backside really well,' De Sousa smiles.

Della Rossa steps back to avoid the splash. He glances down his long nose at De Sousa, tossing him an arrogant snigger.

Zico pushes his upper body out of the cavity, gasping for air. *How can I fix this?* He raises his hands to the sky, praying for a miracle.

A beautiful, bright red paper plane appears from Precious Above the Sea. It gracefully circles the sky. Zico releases the greatest sigh of relief ever. He squirms his way back into the tight space. The red container is pushed into the pipe as the count reaches 31, 32, 33...

At the bottom of the village, everyone is waiting in suspense for what's coming down the pipe. The council members don't expect the container to come through. When the clock hits 55 seconds, they share devious smiles.

At 59 seconds the red container is caught in the net. Fonso grabs the pole, forcing the official's arm up. The net is raised in the air and whipped around like a victory flag. Sewer water splashes everywhere. The community breaks into song and dance, while the bureaucrats are shocked into silence.

Leaping onto the platform, Zico is on top of the world. He tracks the plane's descent into the Deep Forest. Tilting his head back, he shouts toward the cliff, 'We did it. You're brilliant, Sancia.'

With cheers from the crowd far below reaching the toilet chamber, Della Rossa storms out. He leans over the edge of the courtyard and observes his defeat. The officials hang their heads as disorderly celebrations rage throughout the village.

He squeezes his eyes shut, wanting to rid himself of this filthy vision. *They rigged this! How could these people out-smart me?* Taking a breath, he opens his eyes to glare at the Deep Forest, wondering who betrayed him.

★ ★ ★

The next day, the vote in Roldão's Council about the proposed marina is being televised on cable TV. Several councillors face the opposing parties, led by Fonso and Della Rossa. A wide aisle divides the two sides. Fonso checks his watch and glances at the empty seat next to him. Shaking his head, he pushes himself up and goes in search of Zico.

Outside, in the hallway, Sancia is at Zico's side. They are careful not to be noticed by the lurking reporters.

'I told my father I ratted on him to save the Deep Forest and the village,' Sancia admits.

Blinking his eyes, Zico offers a shaky slow smile, certain he misheard. 'You did what? Are you nuts? What did he say?'

'He didn't like it a bit. My dad never loses. He insisted I witness his defeat.'

'Parents. Go Figure.'

Fonso appears at the doorway, waving them in. As they move toward the chamber, Sancia shares, 'Life goes on. He can't be mad at me for too long, can he?' She bites down on her bottom lip as her eyes search Zico's.

They settle in their seats, the aisle an invisible border between them. A hush falls over the room, crammed with spectators and media. The proceedings commence.

With Nothing Forever's population outnumbering Precious Above the Sea residents by 876, the vote to stop the marina is proposed. The Councillor offers Della Rossa a right to object. Looking straight ahead, jaw clenched, he clutches Sancia's hand and gives it a sweaty squeeze. Then, he shakes his head to the surprise of everyone. Sancia expels a loud gasp, proud of her father's concession. For once, she is lost for words.

Afonso Aloisous Caiman-claw Ruas is sworn in as Mayor of the hillside community. He is swathed in a purple silk sash.

The Chief Councillor is demoralised. 'Why don't you tell us the name of your town?'

Fonso doesn't know what to say; his mind is blank. Zico kicks his foot. He opens his notebook to a page with only two words: *Hope Town*. Fonso's glance becomes a stare. He sits perfectly still, overwhelmed by the significance of these words to his people. Zico prompts action with another swift kick.

With a faltering voice, Fonso utters, 'Hopetown.' He repeats the name with conviction, 'Hopetown.'

The echo has a spirit of its own as it rumbles through the chamber. The councillors shrug their shoulders and proclaim Hopetown the newest town in Roldão.

Sancia rocks her chair backward, peering across the divide to the opposition. She grins at Zico and tosses him a mobile phone charger.

★ ★ ★

Later that day, back at Hopetown, Zico's family arrives from the farm. Stepping out of the car, they are greeted by Fonso, Zico, and Sancia. Zico's parents stare timidly at the cable car, the colourful village and its Candomblé possessed, wild dancing people.

Their eyes fall on Zico. The reunion is awkward. Nobody wants to make the first move. Finally, they notice Sancia whose smile welcomes them. At first, they are bewildered, then they embrace Zico and her.

The noise in the colosseum is deafening. Several people are dressed as Orishas, the spirits representing the forces of nature: earth, wind, fire, and water. They dance feverishly. In response, the mob wants to be conquered by the spirits which then act as their protectors. It is playful, intense, and engaging. Perching high above, watching from the VIP balcony, Zico, his parents, and Sancia are in awe.

A sashed-up Fonso, with a rifle in hand, appears at the railing. He fires a shot into the air and a hush falls over the crowd. Everyone jostles into position, craning their necks for a better view of their mayor.

'My fellow citizens. It's time to farewell my grandson. Zico lived as an outsider in the community, but departs as an honorary member of Hopetown.' A thunderous roar rings out and everyone stomps their feet.

Waving his hands in front of him, Fonso calms his people.

He spots Della Rossa, lurking on the fringe. Their eyes meet for a split-second, and they nod their respect to each other.

Fonso signals for Zico and Sancia to claim their place beside him. 'And so is Sancia!'

Applause booms through the colosseum.

'Zico came here to grow up. He made friends in a world unknown to him. So has Sancia. Both learned no matter where you come from, together we can make things work. They not only accepted us for who we are; they saved us, giving us hope for the future! Long live Hopetown!'

Della Rossa is moved by the unity and passion of these people. He realises his daughter is far more capable than he thought. *What a gift, uniting people to help close the gap between rich and poor.* Della Rossa flashes a brilliant smile.

The celebration swells with the crowd cheering and dancing even more intensely.

Captivated by the sights and sounds of a community rejoicing, time seems to stand still. Fonso and Zico's parents talk for a long while, hugging often whilst Zico and Sancia take care of his baby sister.

Sancia pulls funny faces, tickles, and kisses Taís. She is rewarded with nonsensical jabbering and laughter. Zico brings her back to reality, 'Don't be fooled by her giggles and dribble. She behaves horribly when she wants attention!'

'Sounds like you,' she laughs. 'From what you're telling me, Taís has a lot in common with you.'

Before he can respond, Fonso clasps Zico's shoulder with his strong hand. 'It's time to go, Zico.'

'Already?' Zico asks.

'It's okay, Zico.' Sancia reaches out to hold his hand. She surprises him with a quick kiss on the cheek, followed by a thump on the shoulder. Giggling light-heartedly, she says, 'Take care of yourself, Zico. I will miss you.'

Zico waves the mobile phone. 'No, you won't, because I'll hassle you every day.'

'And I'll make sure my next holiday is not in Aspen or Sydney. I'll be visiting you,' she lightly punches his shoulder again, 'in the Amazon.'

Zico's face lights up like a Christmas tree. 'You'll do that? For real?'

'I'd love to unless you have other plans.'

'No plans, just a lot of mischief,' Zico promises.

'Count me in,' she laughs.

Fonso nods to his security detail, who hand him two unique signs: *Zico's Hideout* and *Sancia's Way* . He presents the signs to them.

Fonso says, 'Thanks to you, we might have created an industry that can sustain Hopetown economically. Those street signs, numbers, and letterboxes — everyone wants them. How crazy is that?'

With his arm around Zico's shoulders, Fonso says, 'Because of you and Sancia, our community will thrive. Farewell Zico. Off you go. Remember, I want to see you here next holidays! Unless, of course, you have a better place to go.'

'Thanks, Fonso. But I'll spend the next holiday at home with my family. Sancia too.' Zico stuns his parents. 'The one after, I promise, I'll be back here.'

Zico throws his arms around Fonso and whispers, 'I'm going to tell you the whole truth. You gave me the freedom to fail, and I really stuffed up! I learned a lot about myself from my mistakes. Thank you for your trust.'

Fonso scruffs Zico's hair. 'In saving Hopetown, you saved yourself.'

Fonso, Zico, his parents, and Sancia, group hug before the family leaves the colosseum. Zico turns back and winks.

★ ★ ★

Earlier that day...

In the Deep Forest at the Bay of Plenty, Zico, Sancia, and Boondi form a tight circle.

'I Zico, gatekeeper to the unknown, spinner of truth, and bruised in battle...'

'I Sancia, seeker of adventures, head in the clouds, and slightly overdressed at times...'

Uniting their voices to speak as one, they proclaim, '...name the village, Hopetown.' Boondi roars his satisfaction as they leap into the air in celebration.

CPSIA information can be obtained
at www.ICGtesting.com
Printed in the USA
BVHW092029021121
620550BV00018B/1175